ONE SMALL LIFE

ONE SMALL LIFE

Anna Housego

For Evie, for innocence, for hope.

1

They said she would get used to it, but it'd been two weeks since Grace had travelled downriver to work at the orchard and still the stink caught in her nostrils. The brew that fed apricot, apple and pear trees was made in the shark pit, where chunks of the hapless creatures were layered with soil and left to rot for weeks before the fertiliser was spread to boost the sandy loam.

Corpses. Decay. The worms took it down into the earth so it could emerge as plump fruit for the summer harvest. It was enough to do Grace's head in, that anything dead could ever come to something good.

It had been different the day she'd left to start her job. As the ferry pulled away from the Hobart wharf and headed south, the air had never seemed fresher or the water more alive with sparkle and shine.

She'd ignored the mountain brooding at her back and fixed her sights on the spreading harbour and wide run of the River Derwent. Despite the chill, she had stayed at the rail, resolute with her gaze, to watch all she had known in her seventeen years slip away.

The ferry rocked past Kangaroo Bay and Bellerive Beach, where she and the other girls had been taken for occasional Christmas picnics. As she glanced along the sweep of sand, her cheeks flared at the memory of walking towards the water near the bluff and the three well-dressed girls who had approached. Grace was seven years old.

The tallest girl held out her hand. 'Would you like a chocolate?'

Grace thought she'd never seen anything as beautiful as the shiny gold foil in the girl's palm. She took it with thanks and unwrapped it, her mouth ready for the silky, melting treat. Inside was a pebble.

The girls screeched with laughter, chanting 'home girl, home girl' as they ran off. Any pleasure from the remaining picnic day was burned away by the anger at herself for believing that the gift of a happy moment might be her due.

Grace had never been beyond the farthest bluff, and as the ferry swung wide into the broader reach of the river, she took a deep breath and tried hard to take in so much that was new. On the left, bare hills remained battle-scarred, their timber sacrificed long ago to keep whaling pots boiling. Opposite, across the vast expanse of water flowing from snow melt deep in the wilderness, grand homes and double-storey mansions were neatly stacked in rows up the hillside at Sandy Bay.

She shivered in the south-westerly but didn't seek out the shelter of the cabin. She needed the bite of the wind, the smack of the bow as it slapped through the chop, the river breathing in and out with the swell.

Grace had no memory of her arrival as a baby, but it was no concern because this was the birth that mattered, the one where the river carried her to a fullness of life that could be bent and shaped through quick wits, hard work and seizing any advantages thrown up by chance.

It wasn't that she'd been mistreated at the Salvation Army Rescue Home, but the rules and the repetition had crowded in — morning prayers; Holy Scriptures in the evenings; lessons in arithmetic, writing, reading; training in cooking and laundry work. Lining up in winter for cod liver oil, and in summer, taking turns combing out the hair lice.

It had been an effort at times to have a single independent thought; always a cough in a bed nearby or a rush to load your plate before the meat ran out, and never mind any dawdling when you got your one turn in the bath a week.

Towards the end of every autumn, Matron would call her to the front of the dining room, and Grace was always happy to be singled out. One glorious burst of light after interminable days of grey.

Each step towards Matron had its own measure, the pressure of her left heel on the timber floor, the roll of her foot, the point of balance on the toes before the right heel came forward to take its turn. No hurry, stretching the pleasure, making it worth waiting another whole year. Then standing before Matron, hands clasped low in front to quiet the quivering.

'Your father's sent money for winter boots. See Mrs Webster after lessons and she'll take you into town to get them.'

Grace would hold the moment close, unable to turn away, needing to be instructed to resume her seat.

How she longed for months beforehand for Matron's call. It marked her as someone. She was a girl who had a father, and even better, a father who cared.

Most of the permanents had mothers who were dead or destitute and fathers long gone or in jail. Her friend Rachael's mother had died and the father was blind and had made no contact since the day he handed her over. Though at least Rachael knew that much.

Florence and Rose Underwood sat in the same row as Grace in class and the sisters had no information about their start in life. They didn't even know their own birth dates.

Not Grace. She had a father — who sent money.

Each pair of new winter boots had a pleasing weight that anchored her to the ground. They warmed her heart as much as her feet on the way to church on Sunday mornings. If she'd understood the concept of joy, she might have recognised it in the sweet shiver that sometimes ran up her spine when she glanced at the leather and laces.

The autumn after she turned ten, the frosts set in early. As usual for the season, she lingered each morning after breakfast, waiting to hear the money had arrived.

It never did.

This was the year the earth seemed to pause in its rotation then begin spinning the opposite way. It was the only explanation she had for the fact that, from that time, the days unfolded in their usual monotony yet nothing around her looked the same.

She'd asked about her mother back when she'd become old enough to join the others in the schoolroom. 'There's no sugar-coating it, Grace. She's dead and you're here and that's all you need to know.'

At least when the money had been coming, she could be certain she had a father who thought of her. She didn't know the colour of his eyes; had no idea about his name, whether he was kind or contrary, where he lived, whether he had ever held her in his arms. The contribution that came each year was all that she knew of the man, but it was proof he was out there and hope of maybe more.

When the money stopped, a strange sensation rose in

Grace — a darkness in her chest that spread like the slow stain of candle wax, sticking to her insides for days. And when the heaviness ebbed away, it took something with it. Grace was still attentive in lessons, worked hard in the laundry, read bedtime stories to the younger girls, but her voice was quieter, her breath a little more shallow.

As the years passed, she had grown tall and what little story she had about who she was had stretched thin. In the becalmed hours of early morning, she would lie awake, sick to the stomach, afraid that when daylight arrived she would swing her feet onto the floor to start the day, only to find she had not enough story to stand on.

When there was no ground on which to pitch your past, it was hard to conceive of a future, she admitted to herself as the ferry groaned and swayed its way south. Now, though, she must look to what could begin unfolding, free from the walls and doors of the old boundaries.

She set her eyes downriver. Let the big world come to meet her small life. She would be the one to tell it who she really was.

The ferry left the houses behind and rounded the bend at Droughty Point, with Grace still clinging to the rail, her face damp with spray and her eyes fixed on the horizon as the vessel laboured south towards the fishhook of land known as South Arm Peninsula.

Within minutes, the weather cut up completely and Grace retreated into the cabin. As she stepped over parcels and bags to a seat, she saw cattle swaying and stumbling in a tight pack on the rear deck, heads down to keep the icy spray from their eyes. She was cold by the time the South Arm jetty appeared, barely visible through the storm.

The deckhand poked his head into the cabin. 'Won't

be long. We can't land the cattle so we just have to sort that and we'll be alongside before you know it.' With that he was gone, just as the skipper slowed the vessel.

The deckhand released the side gate and Grace saw him raise a thick stick, forcing one beast after another over the side and into the churning water.

'Oh,' she gasped, as one hand flew to her mouth.

A woman seated nearby leaned over, patting her shoulder. 'It's okay, love. They swim to the beach, they always do. Not like sheep, their wool makes them too heavy and they sink, but this lot'll be okay.'

The dark shapes disappeared one by one.

On the jetty, Grace bent into the driving rain and followed the line of drays waiting for the ferry to be unloaded. The last one had Farley's Orchard in neat letters on the side. The driver made no effort to climb down when she introduced herself. He was older than her, maybe by five years, and unlike the other farm hands was wearing neither a hat nor coat, though that was not what Grace first noticed.

His face was half-turned towards her, and as she glanced up she was prepared for what she had seen the past two summers, working with the other home girls old enough to be harvesting fruit on Derwent Valley farms.

It was a look the farm workers had about them when the girls arrived each morning — the eyes of the young men moving across the face of each girl and then down to her chest and waist, and all the while the lads keeping their heads still as though their brazen appraisals might not be noticed. The men had been clumsy with words, barely speaking, and the girls giggled as they walked off between rows of fruit-laden trees.

This face, however, was different. It had none of the artless glancing of the valley boys. Looking through the blur of rain, she saw only blankness and wondered if he had heard her voice.

All around was strangeness, but as she stood there, rain soaking through her collar, it came to her that this was a familiar feeling. *I am not really here; I do not matter.* Matron's voice scratching its way through the prayer, 'thy will be done, in earth as it is in heaven' — the memory of bowing her head under the weight of it.

It would not do.

Grace straightened and threw her second-hand suitcase onto the dray. *My will, not thine.* Her coat was heavy with the rain as she hauled herself up onto the seat. No sooner was she in her place than the driver jumped off, without a glance in her direction. She watched the stocky fellow, arms thick as tree limbs, lope along the jetty and join the men unloading the ferry. In the months to come, Grace would remember his face and wish to forget the absence of his looking.

With the dray loaded, they rode to the farm in silence. A few minutes from the jetty they turned off, a sign telling her this was Roaring Beach Road. On the left, cleared paddocks gave way to neat lines of fruit trees, while on the right, the land quickly ran into bush that stretched up the only decent hill for miles. The spindly gums and she-oaks were the clue that the slope hadn't been worth clearing.

At the bottom of the straight, the road took a sharp dogleg, and it was there the dray turned off and came to a halt near a weatherboard house that was sulking on a low rise. The house turned its back to the road, instead facing a large packing shed near the edge of the paddock and beyond it, a bunkhouse.

The wind whined in a row of macrocarpa pines on the boundary and above the sound, Graced heard the distant thrash of waves. She scrambled down, uncertain but determined not to show it. *Grace Anderson*, she thought, *your life has begun.*

'You've met Clem, then,' Mrs Farley said as she swung open the back door.

Grace turned back to say hello to the labourer, but he'd already spurred the horse on and was halfway to the shed.

Greta Farley was nothing if not efficient. Within five minutes she had Grace out of her coat and working her way through a tub of dirty dishes.

Grace had expected a few questions at least about her background and skills, and heaven help it, perhaps a pot of hot tea by way of a welcome. Mrs Farley showed no interest whatsoever in anything but keeping up the list of chores to ensure that as fast as Grace finished one job, there was another one lined up. And not even the offer of a glass of water.

A new rhythm began.

It was measured by mornings at the guesthouse run by Rob Farley's spinster sister, Beattie, afternoons on the farm, and in the evenings, what precious free time she had was devoted to soothing walks through the avenues of trees. The order in the orchard appealed to Grace: the carefully planned spacing of the trees in even rows, the way the limbs had been pruned to open to the sun, the reliable pulse of frog calls from the nearby wetlands curled between the farm and sand dunes.

It gave her a sense of ease that not even the fertiliser

stench could overpower and sometimes, as twilight thickened, the orchard seemed a place of great magic. Its bare branches would transform with warm, juice-filled fruit, while the land performed its own remarkable feat, single-handedly holding back the wild Southern Ocean on one flank. On the other, the orchard sprawled across to the isthmus called The Neck, where a shallow tidal bay petered out inside the hook of South Arm and peace prevailed.

Grace liked to think that the flat land of the orchard had everyone fooled but her. To others, it was boring, lacklustre, unlike the sandstone cliffs up the road at Goat's Bluff or the pounding ocean, or the crags and peaks that challenged the sky further south.

She was the one who saw its quiet wizardry, so different to the surging water in the river and bay or the sea's showy play of strength. This was a land that could withstand and surely, she thought, that was a power as mighty as the ocean. Anyone who believed it ordinary was a fool.

Besides, the orchard was the first place she'd ever found where she could rest. Not simply cease activity, which was an easy matter, but be able to quiet the constant whirring within and gently settle. It didn't happen every time she walked the orchard but when it did, she could happily believe in magic.

Peace was certainly not something to be found around Mrs Farley. Grace couldn't say she liked the woman, and it wasn't so much she had a face like a shriveled apple. No, it was those cold eyes following her every move so that she longed to be alone in her small room, a lean-to off the back of the family's house.

It turned out that Clem was helping out while the

eldest son was away for a year with a timber-cutting team. When the lad returned, the plan was for him to work alongside his father and the older farmhand, Jimmy, until his dad retired and he took over the orchard.

The farmer's wife made no bones about what a waste it was to be paying a wage to Jimmy, who'd returned from the Great War with a limp that slowed him down and the lid shut tight on his Army experience.

The younger boy, Teddy, was about eleven and laidback like his father. He was friendly enough with Grace, but it was the eight-year-old daughter she warmed to. She recognised in the girl the hunger for attention and warmth she'd seen in the little ones at the home.

'I'm Elizabeth, but you can call me Lizzy, just don't tell Ma,' she whispered to Grace. On the days when Lizzy sought her out after school and followed her while she did chores, Grace had to admit she was glad to have the lively chatter.

The work was no less relentless at the guesthouse but unlike the arrangement with the farmer's wife, Grace gave her labours willingly to Beattie, who insisted on first names.

Beattie didn't slam out orders like right hooks in a boxing ring but drew forth Grace's efforts through an earthy warmth and a succession of stories. She had a natural rhythm as a storyteller and Grace soon discovered, an uncanny gift for picking up a tale where she'd left off, regardless of stopping mid-sentence to answer the door, call for fresh table napkins or give directions on where to find parsley in the herb garden.

As Grace pounded the bread for its second rising or sliced tomatoes and bacon for guest breakfasts or perhaps set the table in the dining room, her imagination was fed by images of the Iron Pot lighthouse at the river mouth, not far from the orchard.

'You're a few years too late, my dear,' Beattie was telling her one morning while eggs sizzled in the pan. 'The place is just a big rock with not a speck of soil, and still they built a two-storey headkeeper's cottage and a little place for the assistant keeper. Never did such a grand house look so out of place as that one on its barren ground. They pulled it down and carted it away two or three winters back.'

Grace went on toasting thick slabs of bread in front of the fire burning in the cast iron woodstove.

'In '95, I was a bit younger o' course, a southerly buster blew in with a king tide. It was getting dark and as the night came down, that mighty sea had nowhere to go but upriver, and the Iron Pot was all that stood in its way. The headkeeper's wife had a new baby, the only one ever born on the rock, and the waves were going right over the houses and everything was flooding.' Beattie paused, waving the spatula in Grace's direction. 'It must have been terrifying, stuck out there in the fury of the sea and the gale and no way to get help.

'The waves kept pounding in, higher and higher. The water tanks were torn from their mounts and tossed into the river. Didn't matter that they were full. Then they heard the awful grating sound of the stone retaining wall giving way. The houses shook. They knew they were in peril. In the middle of the night, they made a run for it, into the lighthouse.

'They sheltered there till morning, in the teeth of the storm, not knowing if the tower would hold. It's brick and more than sixty feet above sea level, but it would have felt like a flimsy thing on such a night. The two men kept the light going and just before dawn, the wind and the swell died down. When the keeper poked his head out at daylight, there was kelp hanging off the rail alongside the light.'

Grace's head filled with an image of the helpless baby as the storm raged. She hoped it was safe in the mother's arms. Before she could ask any questions, Beattie rushed from the kitchen to greet the schoolteacher, who was the first of the lodgers to come downstairs for breakfast, leaving Grace flooded with strong feelings she couldn't even name.

It was still on her mind as she hurried back to the orchard in the early afternoon. The day before, Beattie had told her about how the lighthouse kids would be rowed to the beach so they could walk to school. While they were having lessons, the headkeeper worked in his vegetable garden above the high tide mark, until he could row them back in the afternoon.

She had pictured the children and the man bobbing in the rowboat, the little ones upright and laughing while their father worked the oars. That scene now gave way to a frightened woman and her crying child, in the dark, waiting.

Except this one came with the eerie sound of screaming wind, the suffocation of water rearing up to assault stone, blackness pressing in against skin, and a chill that clutched at clothes and agitated thoughts so they endlessly circled all through the night.

She heard the thin cry of that wind as she walked back to the orchard, imagining it buffeting the tower while the mother and child cowered inside. As Grace walked, it seemed the howling grew closer, more fevered, and she had reached the dogleg before she realised the high-pitched sound was not in her head but something alive nearby.

She knew that sound. It was a cry of fear.

She was in motion immediately. She sprinted hard to the shed, slowing only to catch her breath at the wide door that was propped open. Inside, she saw Clem Turner and Rob Farley wrestling a lamb.

Her instinct, triggered by the squealing, was to protect it and she stepped towards the men. As she did, Mr Farley raised a large knife and flicked it down in a move that was fast and certain. The sound stopped. Grace froze, unable to turn away or to stop herself from looking, as a thin, red smile appeared on the neck of the lamb.

She was gone before it had turned into a rush of blood down the creature's chest. The men, intent on their task, didn't see Grace peel away.

A rush of emptiness swept away any thoughts or images. Nothing to know but the straining of her lungs, the thud-thud of her boots pumping her body down the dirt road. A blur of fence, bush, water. Sharp cries of alarm from plovers startled into flight at the edge of the wetlands. The dirt turning soft, trying to slow her, calm her, but the fleeing was too strong and the panic shimmery, quick-silver.

Now it was sand and her boots were slipping in the powdery mess and she was kicking to be rid of them. She pushed through low-hanging macrocarpa branches and let them whip her face. Up the side of the dune, she ran, higher and higher.

She burst through the opening at the top of the sandy

ridge, mouth open, sucking in air like a seal returning to the surface after a deep dive. The updraft snapped at her skirt, and then let go. Unable to stop, she tumbled down twenty feet, spinning and twisting to the beach.

Grace lay where she landed, grit in her mouth, ears full of the dull thumping of surf onto wet sand. Her heart ricocheted in her chest, eyes struggling to make sense of a sideways world in a mess of sky-sand-waves-gulls and one strange, close island she soon recognised as her arm.

As her breathing slowed, she pushed herself up to sit with legs folded under her, the heavy cotton skirt still twisted around them, and leaned on one hand.

To her right was the Iron Pot lighthouse, its narrow, red band vivid against white surrounds, and ahead the ocean reared and bucked, rows of dark-green water rising up taller than her and hurling themselves at a steep bench of sand, each line of surf crashing with a roar that had no time to fade before the following one pounded in.

After all the stories, it was not the lighthouse that held her attention but the green, luminescent water, alive and beckoning, reaching out with a promise, but of what? This was not the measured restlessness of the sea that she had known on the river beaches but a raw force from the beginning of time.

She couldn't take her eyes from the walls of glassy green, and as each exhausted itself on the beach in a plume of spray and salt-sting, her eyes searched out the next, and the next.

She wasn't sure how long she'd been sitting there, her mind blank except for the rhythm of the waves, but at last she struggled to her feet, aware that Mrs Farley would be looking for her. As she turned to go, her glance caught the red circle on the lighthouse, bright in the sun; a thin, red line across paleness and everything behind it fading into nothing, while inside her, something unsettling began to rise.

She could run all she liked. It still waited, at her back. It was the strangeness she remembered when she had worked so hard to forget, but remembering was not the right way to describe it, not the right word at all.

She couldn't say it was a memory because there was nothing to see, no frame or shape or recognition of a scene. What came first, its intensity shocking her, was a state that had been suspended all this time, hovering near, always chasing, only ever a breath away.

Some got an unwanted telegram with a knock at the door. Others, a stranger who yanked them back when all they wanted was escape and the right to keep turning and spinning to oblivion.

Grace got a sensation. It gripped her by the shoulders and began shaking gently, back and forth, jerking her head, making it hard to find her centre of gravity.

She knew enough of what it was to be sure of one thing. It would not remain gentle.

2

It was the year the money stopped.

In the eyes of the world she was now an orphan, but when she looked out through the marble blue of her own irises, she saw all the hope that childhood brings in its cocoon. It was easy for Grace as an adult to know it now, of course, but the younger Grace had no idea that there was worse to come. Soon she'd know what it truly meant to be abandoned.

She had been keen to find Mary, one of the older girls at the home, and she'd hurried with a bounce in her step, impelled by purpose and anticipation.

She remembered it now; the tiny treasure her ten-year-old self held in her hand, her heart singing with intent on offering it. It was a Rosella parrot feather with bright colours to impress the older girl and, oh the pleasure of it, to be rewarded with a warm hug.

She'd pushed the door ajar, face hot with excitement, ready for the embrace that she'd come to expect from Mary, who was the closest thing to a mother that Grace had ever known.

Mary was, in fact, the reason Grace had lived at the home all her life, unlike all the other babies fostered out soon after they arrived. 'When you turned up, you were my miracle,' Mary had told Grace many times. Only months earlier and six years old herself, Mary had watched consumption weaken her baby sister until she had faded to nothing.

It was Mary who, in need of nurturing herself, did the next best thing and gave to Grace all that she'd never received. Soon, she had taken over much of Grace's care and softened the urgency to find a placement for the baby. Somehow, as time went by, the Matron never did.

The day of the feather was the day Grace discovered that what seemed solid could fragment in an instant. Ice could crack a boulder. Rust could disintegrate metal to dust. A small thing, just the opening of a door, and all that was known could disappear.

She could still feel it in her veins, even now: the slow dissolving, the sense of her skeleton slipping, and through it all the surprise that as her bones turned liquid she continued to prop herself upright.

Grace had stood in the doorway looking at Mary, but the woman she saw before her was not the one she knew. *Her* Mary laughed and swirled, danced with Grace. Hugged and soothed. Wrapped bumps and bruises in her softness and made them better. Hid extra bits of biscuit and slipped them to her at night.

This one should be Mary yet was not. The face had a familiar outline but was not kind or smiling, and it made no sense to Grace, nor did the fierce heat that rose from her core to unpick her mind.

She squeezed her eyes and strained with the effort of trying to understand. The place between her eyebrows that didn't have a name was beginning to hurt, but still the shapes and objects blurred into ghostly figures.

And then they formed in clear view.

The young woman in Mary's dress, with Mary's wavy, brown hair, stood beside the cot, motionless.

From her arms, like a bundle of paper bunting torn

by the wind at the Christmas fair, the baby hung limp, its limbs askew. Grace saw the dressmaking scissors on the floor; she tried to focus there. Too late, her eyes searched up and found the red line, a lick of crayon spread across the child's throat.

Grace's hand was on the doorknob and she felt the familiar cold of the brass and the smooth roundness of it, but the red thing she couldn't fathom, not even as it flowered open and spilled bright bursts that stained the baby's blanket and dripped onto the floor.

The stiff face moved then and a voice came from it, harsh, demanding. 'Get out, Gracie, get out,' she grunted.

Grace had intended to knock like she mostly did before she went into Mary's room, especially with the arrival of the baby a few weeks earlier. All summer, since the older girls had worked a season on the Derwent hop farm, Mary's belly had swollen and Grace had thought this was a good thing.

Who cared that Matron's mood was stormy and Mary was made to stay behind when they all went to Sunday morning's Divine Service? What mattered was that Mary would not leave the home to go to the job that'd been arranged at the tailor shop in town.

Grace hoped God would forgive her for her selfishness and the pleasure at Matron's plans coming unstuck, but if she was a bad person, surely God would not have made it such a happy time. She not only had Mary, but now the baby girl, with her sweet smell and delicate fingers and toes.

'We can't keep her,' Mary had murmured the evening before, when Grace said goodnight. 'They'll find her a new mother and send me away.'

She'd gone to bed, not understanding anything of the

older girl's desperation. Had got up to a new day, giving herself freely to its routines — until the feather.

She was still rooted to the spot when Mrs Webster came down the corridor, pushing Grace aside and screaming for help. Grace stayed there, her back against the wall, its hard surface the one certain thing in the pandemonium that followed.

It must have taken some time before the police arrived, but she remembered nothing, except Mrs Webster pinning her down and the wildness of the animal thrashing in her, fists and heels banging on the floor, as Mary was led out between the two officers.

Matron followed the men and their stumbling prisoner out to the front step and shut the door behind them, a gesture that came to mean she'd closed down the subject of Mary or any subject, for that matter, that might get close to it.

Grace thought it had all been given over to another time, a forgetting that had come to bless her in the pain, the longing, all the weeks of bewilderment. She'd been fooling herself.

A sharp gust of wind tugged at her hair, dragging her back from the past, and in that instant, standing on the beach, every part of Grace ached. A membrane of hurt stretched tight below her skin. She wanted to pierce it like a boil, to have it drain, bleed out onto the sand. She wanted to damn Mary, wish her to hell, but she was grown up now and understood one thing that she hadn't back then. If hell was a place, Mary was already there.

She looked away from the lighthouse and scanned the sky. The sun had gone behind streaks of cloud and the surf was now dull grey.

Hope Beach was its name, Beattie had said, not because

of the possibility of anything at all but named after a shipwreck, its bones joining the many vessels claimed by the ocean before they could make it into the river mouth.

Rumours had swirled for years that the regimental payroll, 20,000 pounds in gold, had been in the hold, and the Ensign and a couple of soldiers had made off with it.

Shielding her eyes with one hand, Grace looked past the blunt top of nearby Betsey Island. Good luck to them. She had no desire for gold.

Ships from foreign ports, from Antarctica, they all braved this ocean to make it up the Derwent to the harbour. What she yearned for was the chance to be on one of them, in the churning and tossing, rising and plunging, feeling the rage of the water and the danger of it.

She would let it decide where she needed to go, let it take her far from Mary, Matron, from the baby who would never grow. From the father who stopped caring. The orchard wife who snarled and snapped. She would leave the days of drudgery, the shore, the entire unhappy island. She would meet the swelling tide and it would take her.

The south-westerly was turning bitter and she was trembling and cold.

She took one last look at the breakers and scrambled awkwardly up the dune, not bothering to brush the wet sand from her skirt when she reached the top. She found her boots, pushed her feet into them and trudged in the direction of the farmhouse.

Near the bunkhouse where the farmhands slept, she caught sight of a small movement. She thought it was Clem but when she turned to face him, there was only the side wall and the corner post on the fence and in between them, air.

3

The days were getting shorter and soon Grace knew there wouldn't be enough light for her walk in the evening, the one time of day that was hers. It marked the end of chores but not yet the hour that she would turn in to bed, a reprieve from the burden of knowing that soon it would be dawn and she'd have to start all over again.

She hurried away from the house before Mrs Farley could ask her to do one more thing, and with twilight closing in, she took a shortcut through the bottom paddock where the house cow grazed.

Intent on making the most of the remaining daylight, Grace skirted the new shark pit, pleased that the layering of flesh and soil had only been completed that week and the smell hadn't yet had time to take hold.

The second pit was another matter. It had been made the previous spring and the mix had been left to break down for six months into a rotting soil-soup. She held her nose against the powerful odour and looked down at her feet to make sure she didn't slip on the sloping rim.

A shape sprang out of the gloom and before she had time to register what was happening, the figure shoved hard against her shoulder and she skidded towards the pit. The mess was spongy under foot but not sloppy, and for a moment she thought maybe she hadn't gone in because she didn't go under.

It was then she felt herself sinking and the shock

and panic hit. She thrashed her way to the lip of the pit, working the festering muck into her hair, through her clothes and into her boots.

She heard Clem laugh. He waited, not attempting to help, while she clambered out, spluttering and reeking of decay.

'Stupid thing to do. It's not funny. What was that for?' she shouted, shaking both fists in his direction.

He strolled away, without saying a word.

As she neared the house she was fuming about the clean-up she'd need and about missing out on the one private joy in her day. Mostly, though, she was furious about the senselessness of it.

In her room, stripping off her blouse, skirt and boots, she shivered as she remembered him staring at her, silent and still, a feral cat sizing up a baby rabbit. She pushed the thought aside, working hard to keep it out on the edges and all the while waiting for sleep to wipe it out and save her the effort.

The next evening, as she helped serve the meal in the Farley's kitchen, she was grateful the two farm workers ate in the bunkhouse and she didn't have to look at Clem across the table.

She was a strong woman, she kept telling herself, and wouldn't fall for another practical joke from the likes of him. She'd known worse during her time at the home and working on farms the past two summers — men who thought it a lark to tease or give you a fright, who got pleasure from hearing you squeal or seeing you startle and freeze.

Later, in her room, she caught herself listening to the noises outside, straining to recognise the sound of each insect banging on the window, each cricket or frog signaling through the chill. She thought for a moment she could smell a smoky, stale body odour but quickly dismissed it.

Slow to fall asleep, she lay on her back and reminded herself that this was part of finding her own way, that she could handle what life threw in front of her.

She would become a woman who was more than shame; she would show them she was not someone who needed others to look after her. She'd carried the abandoned child far too long. It was time to lay down the load and make herself into someone capable.

She rolled over to face the window, reining in her mind every time it went back to the shark pit. She kept her eyes open for as long as she could, preferring the soft gloom of the moon filtering through the curtains to the darkness behind her eyelids.

Grace was churning butter the next afternoon, or at least trying to, when she heard the fuss. The plunger kept jamming and she'd been quietly cursing, yet again, Mrs Farley's refusal to buy one of the new models with fancy internal paddles that halved the time it took.

Lizzy was shouting as she ran down the road from school with two friends, Teddy trailing behind. 'There's a whale washed up on Hope Beach. Come quick, Grace, let's go see.' They tossed their satchels into the back porch.

'You go on, Lizzy, I've got things to finish for now,' she called out to the girl, already halfway back to the road. About an hour later, the butter was in the coolbox and she had the chance to slip away.

The surf had dumped the whale on its back and its great bulk had compressed the sand, as though it was sinking into the beach. Grace has seen photos of humpbacks in her schoolbooks but she wasn't prepared for the heft of it, the body as long as the trams that trundled up Elizabeth Street from the GPO. More astonishing, its belly was marked with slashes from the chin almost to the tail, reminding her of the way a fork dragged across mashed potato on a shepherd's pie.

Grace was speechless before the ancient creature. There had been a time when whales swam freely in the river and the ocean; yet they'd all ended up in the blubber pots well before she'd been born.

'They sing, you know,' Jimmy said quietly. 'You'll get sailors, after a few drinks, who'll tell ya about hearing the crying and the sweetness of the humming that goes on for hours at sea. Brings some of those old fellas to tears.'

Grace could only nod. In its massive presence, she couldn't find a single word big enough to utter that would do it justice. It was wrong that it had been stranded on its back, and her impulse was to try to roll it over but it was clear it was useless to attempt it and foolish to share such a thought with Jimmy.

For a brief moment she considered praying for it to be swimming again in the sea, but then she'd known since she was ten that praying was a waste of good breath. *I hope your god takes more care than mine.*

She longed to stay with the whale. A messenger from the deep, it had come for her, she was convinced of it. It did nothing, shared nothing. She didn't even reach out a hand, though she felt its touch just the same, and for a moment it seemed to rise a little and move, until she realised it was just the teary film across her eyes.

Work was waiting and she took one last look at the

whale, stuck fast while the sea frothed and surged, and then she followed Jimmy as he slowly worked his way back up the dune. She took deliberate breaths, drawing in oxygen-rich air that filtered through her lungs into every cell. Here was a place where she felt more alive than anywhere, on this beach with a swelling tide and towering rows of green water rolling in. Maybe, she thought, it was a clue — a shaky connection to her origins.

She must have come from somewhere, been formed by a particular set of facts. Perhaps she'd been born by the sea, under a wide sky. She pictured a grassy clearing above the high tide mark and a tiny cottage, smoke rising from its one chimney while seagulls wheeled lazily above.

She tried to imagine a mother at the door wearing a flour-dusted apron and a soft smile, watching for her husband to return from his day's work. Inside, a contented baby girl was dozing in her cradle. She pictured the gravel path winding to the door, felt the pull of how much she wanted to walk it and arrive at the end. But try as she might, she couldn't conjure up the mother, while the father had long since fled, covering his tracks as he went.

She should know better than to entertain such childish thoughts. It was all so long ago, what did it matter now? And anyway, the waves at Hope Beach didn't soothe her or provide the sense of calm you'd expect if they spoke of her birthplace. Not even the rhythmic roar at night of the wind-driven surf heaving itself onto the sand, distant from her bed, gave her any peace.

No, she was alive before that ocean because it had power, because it was so utterly unknown and she, Grace, was nothing more than a tiny speck of sand it was waiting to claim. Strange how that comforted her, the understanding that the sea could swallow her in an instant and take her for its own.

She chided herself for thinking that way and turned her attention to practical matters at the farm, before leaving late morning for a shift at the guesthouse. The approach to it never failed to lift her spirits.

It wasn't only Beattie who welcomed her but the house itself. It crouched on the one elevated piece of land above Half Moon Bay, a grey, weathered guard dog, alert, haunches spreading, watching over the smattering of structures that made up the town. Its upper verandah surveyed houses, a couple of shops, the school, hall and sports oval. From the ground floor a well-worn path kept it leashed to the jetty, beach and a nearby swimming pontoon.

The weather had made an early dip into spring, and several of the shack families had arrived on the morning ferry for the weekend. A gaggle of young women, not much younger than Grace, came laughing into the dining room. They wore shorts pulled over damp bathers, a dusting of sand clinging to fine hairs covering arms and legs.

She marveled at their casual manner and the easy way they joked with each other. Their beach was a place of play and lightheartedness, but Grace could only think of the wild sweep of sand on the ocean side of the peninsula, where the sea had thrown up a whale that lay lifeless and stranded. While the girls chattered, Grace served their food without smiling.

The guesthouse was unexpectedly busy and she stayed late to help with gravy-stained dishes and several roasting pans. She slipped into the dining room without being asked, sweeping sand from the floorboards before Beattie had a chance to bemoan the damage the grit did to the waxed finish.

She put the broom away and tugged off her apron. It didn't matter to Mrs Farley if there'd been extra to do for lunch guests — she'd still expect the washing off the line and Grace to finish whatever list of chores she'd drummed up.

Beattie came into the kitchen more slowly than usual. 'Before you go, Gracie, I just want to let you know I've asked Greta to let you do a trip to town on Monday for my shopping. My feet can't take it anymore.'

Grace had noticed Beattie's arthritic feet were a strange shape, the toes twisted so that the ends of her shoes had worked themselves into an upward curl, but hadn't thought anything of it. She was ashamed she'd been so caught up in her own world that she hadn't noticed Beattie was in pain.

'But Monday's washing day, Beattie, I don't know if Mrs Farley will let me go.'

She hadn't meant to blurt out the challenge, but the sudden awareness of Beattie's condition and the unexpected treat of a day in Hobart had thrown her.

'Don't you worry about that, Gracie. She's already agreed. We know you can find your way around the streets, and no doubt you can pick up a few things for her while you're there.'

On the road back to the farmhouse, Gracie skipped along the straight like a five-year-old, not caring who might see. She promised herself, by way of celebration, that she would get up early and go visit the whale.

Hours later in her room, she slipped on her cotton nightie and laid her clothes out on a chair so she could dress quickly at first light. The thought of the whale, belly exposed, made her shudder with the thrill of another encounter.

The creature may be dead but it had breathed in a saltwater world, dived through the thrust and pull of tides, roamed with ocean currents far from land. To stand on the beach with it was to know something of what lay past the horizon. It had seen things Grace could never hope to and she longed to be with it on her own, as though being in its presence might draw out something waiting to bloom in her.

Next morning, as she climbed the dune, the magpies were beginning their caroling even though the sun was slow to break free from the lip of the sea. The tide was out, revealing a steep ramp of sand, packed hard by the receding surf.

The beach was empty.

Grace scanned the sand in both directions but there was nothing. The whale was gone.

She registered her disbelief. Such a huge animal, how could it have been swept away? She shoved the back of her hand across her cheek to wipe away a tear and sniffed hard to stop more from flowing. It was absurd to feel so much for the creature. It owed her nothing, yet the loss was a solid thing in her belly, rising to tighten her throat.

She looked again up the length of the beach and as she did, the reality became clear. The ocean had the whale back in its keeping.

In the darkness, while she had been sleeping, the rippling muscle of the sea had carried the whale from her and left no sign that it ever existed.

The realisation was a weight, so Grace sat heavily in the spinifex, ignoring the spikes digging into her calves.

The day ahead taunted with its certain load of work, to be followed by the same again the next day and the day after, forever more.

The beach had betrayed her. Like so much else.

She forced herself to stand before the self-pity buried her. She scuffed the sand with her heels and watched them sink like the whale, fighting the urge to keep digging until the beach took all of her in, sand filling her ears, eyes and nose. She would stretch her mouth wide, and then wider still, letting it flow in to the brim. Filling her with salt and sun-heat, fragments of shells and bones. Drawing her into the immensity of the dunes, ready for the storm that would come, maybe not for a few winters, a decade or even a century, but it would surely come and release her in the way it had the whale.

The thought eased her misery and she leaned down to brush damp sand from her skirt, though it was much harder to fend off the wanting that wouldn't leave her alone. Her limbs dragged with weariness as she left the dunes but at least she was moving.

She crossed the wetlands on the road and then climbed the fence, taking a direct route back to the house, along the rows of apple trees. A swamp harrier glided overhead and she watched it go by, then pause, before it shot like an arrow into the edge of the reeds.

Turning back towards the house, she spotted Clem leaning against the new spray pump rig, slowly raising a cigarette to his lips while he stared at her. As soon as he saw her looking, he bent down and busied himself adjusting the flywheel.

She quickened her step and passed by with barely a nod in his direction, not giving him the satisfaction of checking to see if he was following. As she entered the kitchen, it was a relief to be back within reach of Mrs Farley's scalding tongue and listening to Lizzy and Teddy argue about whose turn it was to cook the toast.

On Monday as she approached the jetty, the *Cartela* was still labouring across the river, steaming low in the water with its load of timber from small sawmills down the D'Entrecasteaux Channel. Despite the shopping list in her purse and a head full of instructions, Grace's step was light. The rare gift of a whole day to herself had been unimaginable a week ago. Now her pores opened to take it in.

Mrs Farley and Beattie had paid her wages and Grace decided that today was the day she'd buy her first new dress. Blue, like the wide sky floating high over the beach, water and distant hills. It was a good sign that the river was calm despite a stiff breeze.

It took the ferry nearly an hour to chug upriver, stopping at small jetties along the way before reaching the harbour, arms flung wide to the city. The port was crawling with activity as wagons fanned in from the city centre, bringing supplies for three vessels flying foreign flags Grace didn't recognise.

As she stepped off the ferry at Brooke Street Pier, she saw a small crowd gathered on the opposite wharf, where a thin cloud of steam hovered above four mysterious grey shapes.

She began walking towards the city centre, intent on the shopping to be done, but after a few minutes, circled back. *Who will know? Today I can do things my way.* She skirted the crowd and approached a sailor standing to attention near a gangplank that dropped out of sight. Ropes swung from bollards down to four submarines tethered together, a stranded pod of sea creatures.

A few men were at work on the flat upper decks of the vessels and on one, a hatch was open and a sailor sat on the edge, his feet dangling inside the vessel. The nose of each submarine sat flush with the waterline and the deck rose up from there to the conning tower at the rear.

Grace was awestruck. 'What's it like when you dive down?'

The uniformed fellow maintained his stiff position, legs apart and arms folded behind his back. He barely moved his lips. 'Like being in a bathtub, Miss, except the water's on the outside.'

Grace threw her head back and laughed. 'Do you get seasick when you're in one?'

He winked in reply and then lowered his voice. 'Not officially. But between you and me, she rolls and pitches quite bad so it happens all the time.'

It was a conundrum to Grace that the vessels floated so lightly, heavy metal structures swaying gently with the backwash from passing ferries. She imagined climbing down inside the belly of one, going below the waterline into darkness. 'Can I look inside?'

The sailor stayed at attention, staring ahead. 'The public will be allowed to go through on Saturday.'

She was crestfallen. It was difficult enough to get to the city for one day and there would be no return journey on the weekend. She turned to leave.

'You can come back when I finish work and I'll give you a personal tour,' he said under his breath. He was looking at her this time and there was something cool in the appraisal that reminded her of Clem.

For a moment, she froze. A heavyset man pushed past her to the edge of the wharf, breaking the spell, and she fled.

By the time she'd reached the GPO, its clock was striking ten o'clock and she'd recovered her sense of freedom. She hurried towards Fitzgeralds Emporium in search of the catalogue items Mrs Farley had requested.

From there, one shopping bag already full, she went to Brownells department store. She had forgotten how vast it was and it took a moment to get her bearings. Haberdashery for Lizzy's school ribbons, children's wear for socks, manchester for pillowcases for the guesthouse. She made a mental note to stop next at the specialty grocer for Beattie's oolong tea and the spicy sausage that was a favourite of one of the guesthouse regulars.

In the women's section she was captivated by the central display, an ivory full-length wedding dress on a tall mannequin. The high neckline was edged with delicate lace, matching the trim on the softly gathered sleeves. The dress fell in narrow pleats from the waist, brushing the floor at the front but cleverly continuing in cascading folds that formed a mock train at the rear.

Grace thought it the most beautiful dress she'd ever seen. She read the swing tag: House of London. *Out of your league, my girl.*

As she wandered over to the ready-to-wear racks, a salesgirl approached. She wasn't much older than Grace but wore artful makeup with smoky eyes, and her hair had been crimped into waves that cascaded from a side part.

It was clear the girl thought Grace was a drudge.

'Can I help you, Madam,' the young woman said, overdoing her politeness to underscore her superiority.

Grace's natural instinct, well practised at the Salvation

Army home, was to make herself small when she heard that particular tone. Her body was already curling in on itself, head dropping, chest hollow, hands clutching each other through the tangle of her shopping bags.

Her posture of insignificance emboldened the haughty girl. The assistant pressed forward, mouth pursed, sucking the joy from Grace's day, a tall version of the vacuum cleaner that made short work of soot when the salesman showed it to Mrs Farley.

This simply will not do. Her own voice came to the rescue, prodding so firmly within that Grace wondered why the girl hadn't heard it.

Grace drew herself up and looked the woman in the eye. 'I'm after a dress, something special. Of course, I see you're busy so if you're unable to help me, I'm happy to browse on my own.'

The salesgirl rose to the challenge.

Ten minutes later, Grace was in the change room wearing nothing but her petticoat and a grin. Three delicious blue dresses were draped over the chair. She slipped a pale-blue one over her head and turned to the mirror. The wide collar was edged in navy piping, as were the slanted pockets on the skirt.

The woman in the mirror looking back was one Grace hadn't seen before: her thick hair was still a little wild but the fitted dress made her look quite smart. The soft fabric brushed her calves pleasantly as she turned for a full view.

The next dress had a pretty floral pattern but was a thicker cloth, stiff against her skin. She could hear Matron's opinion, clear as a bell. 'Much more hard-wearing. That one will last.' Grace yanked it off quickly, leaving it inside out as she tossed it on the chair.

The third one, with tiny, white polka dots and a line of white buttons down the bodice, was light and hugged the contours of her breasts and hips. *To hell with Matron and the shopgirl.* She would buy this one.

Her shopping bags bulged with the morning purchases, a handle on the straw one fraying with the strain. It was time to head back to the ferry terminal, where she could leave the first round of parcels.

She still had Teddy's books to buy and they would be heavy — thick ones ordered by the teacher who was coaching him for next year, when he started as a senior at the grammar school up north. Like it or not, his father had decided he was destined for the law and would continue with his schooling. Grace comforted herself with the thought, as she hurried downhill, that at least she didn't have that pressure to live up to.

Returning towards Liverpool Street, parcels safely stored and anticipating the cream bun she would order at the teashop, she paused at the Palace Theatre. The curved awning sheltered a beckoning entrance with steps leading to a dim interior.

Lillian Gish looked out at her from a poster, while a handsome mustachioed Army officer lifted the beauty's hand to his lips. The actress was composed, holding his attention. Grace studied her hair, her steady gaze, the way she held her face towards the man.

The theatre was still showing *The Ten Commandments*, but Grace only gave the poster a cursory glance. *I know how that one turned out.*

'Want to join me for the one o'clock?'

She jumped. Swinging around, she faced the submariner from the docks and his mates behind him, hands in pockets. 'My shout, of course.'

The men were laughing, jostling each other, rowdy with the freedom of an afternoon off. They pretended not to notice their friend's invitation, but Grace could see they were cheering him on.

She blushed, the burst of courage from staring down the shopgirl now gone.

The sailor was barely taller than her but she felt small alongside him and the others. The empty straw bag was in her hand and she pulled it over her arm, drawing it in front of her as she did.

'Come on, it'll be fun.' He didn't wait for her reply but reached over and gripped her elbow, guiding her up the stairs.

The hand on her arm was firm and without meaning to, she was led through the entrance. Over the sailor's shoulder she caught sight of one of the men raising his eyebrows, his mate nodding in response. The men gathered behind her and the group swept up the stairs, carrying her along, the sailor still holding her elbow.

When they fronted at the ticket window, the middle-aged woman behind the counter took her time pulling tickets from the roll, unimpressed by the interlopers. Grace had never seen the inside of the theatre and it was a plush cavern. The foyer was vast, stairs rising to one side adding to the grandeur.

In other circumstances, she might have gushed in admiration or taken her time admiring the deep maroon on the walls and the glittering ceiling. But all she noticed was the trembling in her legs and the need to be anywhere else but with the men.

She'd felt it many times before, the blanket of deadness

and calm that fell over her at unpredictable moments. She wasn't in church, she knew that, but she may well have been; caught in the pause before the sermon when the coughing and shuffling subsided as the Reverend stood to speak and thick silence descended.

The sailors' voices didn't penetrate the dull state; she was absent in her quiet cocoon. She heard a bell ringing to signal patrons to their seats. She counted three rings — at least she thought it was three.

She glanced back at the queue forming rapidly behind them, as though looking through a window. Housewives and a few shift-workers shuffled forward, all with a reason to be there. One woman stared at her and then glared pointedly at the sailors.

It was then that the final bell rang. It shattered any sense of glass, and with a jolt, Grace saw and heard everything around her.

A hot charge of blood rushed through her chest and she broke away, awkward and stumbling towards the open doors.

'Hey you, what about the movie?'

She heard the outrage in his shout before she reached the street. She bolted two blocks, turning left then right before she risked looking back. There was not a single sailor's cap in sight but she felt skittish just the same and had to check twice to remember what street she was in.

The cream bun didn't seem so appealing; she needed to stay on the move.

At the bookshop, the assistant knew the titles on her list and disappeared to the education section of the store. When he returned to the counter, he had three hefty books in his hands. 'Someone's trying to get ahead. *Modern First*

Year Algebra, Collar and Daniell's First Year Latin, Roget's Thesaurus. You're a brainy one.' His manner was gently teasing as he began wrapping the books.

'You might be surprised,' Grace snapped back, at once ashamed of her rudeness. He was not the one to blame for her encounter with the sailors.

She kept her head lowered on the walk along Elizabeth Street to the hardware store, where she bought six rubber rings for preserving jars. Next stop was Davern's Chemist for a large bottle of the cough medicine they mixed in the dispensary.

By then it was two o'clock and her legs were still shaky. She detoured to 'the Greeks', as it was known despite the sign out the front that said Brittania Café. She requested a pot of tea and thought it best to order something small to settle her stomach. She decided on a crescent pastry dusted with icing sugar.

She would still have time to get to the jeweller for Mrs Farley's repaired wristwatch and make it to the ferry in an hour.

Her table was near the window. Inside, a waiter and two waitresses moved effortlessly between the diners, the counter and the kitchen. Trays of milkshakes, soft drinks, teas, and occasional food sailed by. Outside, pedestrians were striding along footpaths on either side of the street, their faces in profile, intent on their purpose.

More faces passed, framed in the windows of occasional cars and a double-decker tram. A second tram went by and Grace scanned the passengers but didn't recognise a single one. She'd been in the city for four hours and had not seen one familiar soul.

I am utterly alone. The thought stormed in, cold,

blinding. Its presence so bold she glanced around expecting that others could see it loom over her. While she had been learning to tie her shoelaces, do her sums and practise obedience to Matron and God, it had been growing a secret chamber with every heartbeat. The filmy blue dress with white polka dots, waiting with the other parcels at the ferry office, seemed a small consolation.

She drank her tea and was glad to be sitting because she might have fallen down otherwise. The load of it was such pressure on her joints, it might break her apart. Would the cartilage hold?

She looked to her breath; it had not failed her before. It was a relief to find her lungs still expanded then let go in a certain rhythm, though the air rasped on its way in and out, or so it seemed as she shifted on the chair in search of a new centre of gravity.

She'd worked so hard at believing herself a woman owning a place in the world that she'd thought it was real, that perhaps she was wanted, valuable. The foolishness stung, not the one, clean attack from a bee, but repeatedly, a wasp coming at her from all directions.

The hum of the café mocked her — how always her life had been filled with people but they'd only served to disguise the truth that she travelled through her days alone. It'd been different with Mary, of course, but she was locked in a distant past.

The chatter from nearby tables got to her and she roused herself and paid the bill. She took the long way to the pier to avoid the Palace, weaving across several streets and cutting through the rose garden in St David's Park to the waterfront.

As the ferry reversed out of its berth and nosed its way

into the harbour, thick clouds pressed down, squeezing the colour from the river so all that remained was the cold grey of gunmetal. Though Grace strained to see the distant hills, the horizon was non-existent and offered no solid place where she could anchor her eyes. She took a seat inside and stayed there until the ferry approached the Pigeon Holes at the top of Half Moon Bay.

Jimmy was waiting near the jetty with the dray and helped her load the shopping. He wasn't much of a talker but he clucked at the horse and hummed as they passed the guesthouse and turned in the direction of the farm.

Grace closed her eyes as the cart rocked along. When Jimmy tapped her arm she looked in the direction he was pointing, to a nearby eucalypt with spreading limbs, many dead, bleached almost white by the sun.

'Well I'll be damned,' he whispered. 'Look at that, Grace. Never seen one do that before.'

On one of the higher limbs stood a slim, white-faced heron. Usually at home wading in waterways, it was a strange sight perched in the tree, stretching its long neck upright and extending a narrow beak as it balanced on stick-thin legs for no apparent purpose.

'Must think it's a hawk,' he chuckled.

Grace felt sorry for the bird. 'Maybe, Jimmy, it just wants a different view.'

4

Weeks of pruning in the orchard were done and the bonfire from the discarded limbs was a pile of cold ashes. As the days went by, delicate petals opened one by one on the early Moorpark apricots but the blossom would not be in full flurry until spring arrived.

In the outhouse at Beattie's, Grace tried to make no sound as she retched. It wasn't that she didn't want Beattie to hear, though she most definitely didn't; she was desperate to avoid the sound each time she gagged from reigniting the memory of the recent night that she was determined to forget.

For days she'd been careful to eat as usual with the Farleys or with Beattie so she didn't attract attention, but each time she'd had to fight the pressure of the food at the back of her mouth and in her throat. After the meal she'd flee to the dunny and throw up the food, bile burning her oesophagus and nasal passages.

This new need to purge herself, to get rid of what she'd been forced to take in, was impossible to ignore. Given a choice, she wouldn't have swallowed the food in the first place, wouldn't have let it slide down to reach her stomach. Better still, if she'd had free will in the matter she might have cut her throat out altogether and saved herself the trouble of pretending to eat.

She closed the toilet lid and wiped around the seat to be sure she hadn't left any spatters of undigested lunch.

She took her time levering herself with one arm into a standing position, unsteady from the exhaustion of vomiting.

The day before she'd burned her hand on the stove at the farm and the bandage was still wrapped around her palm and secured to her wrist.

'As if I've got time to be playing nurse,' Mrs Farley had grumbled as she slapped a layer of thick, yellow salve onto the red streak and tied on padding so Grace could go on with her efforts at keeping the fire hot for the potatoes and pumpkin roasting in the oven beneath the coals.

She would have to fall down in a faint before Greta Farley noticed anything was wrong. It had only been the accidental squeal erupting from her when the skin seared that got a response. However, Beattie was a different matter and she had to be more careful around her so she wouldn't start asking questions that Grace might be tempted to answer.

Besides, everything was just fine. She got up at the same hour, did mornings at the farm, a few hours with Beattie, and then returned to the Farleys to help with mending, darning and ironing, cleaning out the chicken coop or lending a hand in the yard.

Over breakfast earlier in the week, Rob Farley had surprised her with a spirited speech about why he was particular about pest control. No way would he be standing in the police court, like a local orchardist the previous season, pleading guilty to a charge of supplying infected fruit to market in England.

'Silly old coot. Time he retired. The inspector found five bushels out of ten cases, makes it bad for all of us. I'll be needing you to give the boys a hand, Grace.'

Grace had cringed at the request and while she had her reasons to refuse, she remained mute as Mr Farley explained how she'd help Clem and Jimmy hang traps for codlin moth in the apple trees. The two farmhands had screwed together short lengths of old fence palings, leaving a small gap between them to attract the moth larvae.

The three of them had walked the orchard, each along a row, hooking a trap on every tree in the hope that when they were removed in three weeks, they'd done their job fooling the grubs and they could be destroyed.

Jimmy gave her the low-down on the picking season to come. Apricots were first, from mid-January, the best ones sold to the local market as fresh fruit and the seconds to the jam factory sprawling along the wharf in Hobart. As that harvest finished, the pickers and packers shifted to the apples.

'The Sturmers, they taste like a lump of wood when they're picked,' Jimmy confided as he took his time rolling a smoke during a break. 'They're good keepers though and by the time they get to London, sweet as sweet.'

At this time of year the apples were still a mystery, forming in twigs and fruit spurs, but Grace could picture them, swollen on drooping branches under a warm sun. She was grateful as Jimmy continued his descriptions of the ripened fruit to come, especially that his attention gave her the excuse to stay close to him.

The Farleys also grew Jonathans for export, 'ruby red and crisp on the bite', as well as Scarlet Pearmains. 'They're the best I reckon. A nice red flush on cream skin and they taste like strawberries. Rob likes 'em because they're prolific croppers.'

With the traps all done, it was a relief when Mrs Farley called her to the side of the house to deal with a sole specimen of Cleopatra, planted when she'd married. It wasn't a variety favoured by Mr Farley, but Grace figured he'd have planted it to keep the peace, given his wife preferred the fruit for pie-making.

Mrs Farley had insisted on her method to capture the moths, and under the woman's close scrutiny, Grace placed an inch or so of molasses in the bottom of a milk bottle and covered it with a cup of cider vinegar and a pinch of ammonia before mixing in water. She tied heavy twine around the neck of the bottle and hung it in the tree.

Yes, there'd been plenty to get on with and Grace had bent her back to the tasks, though had anyone bothered to ask she wouldn't have been able to recall exactly what she'd achieved in the previous week.

She clipped the latch on the outhouse door and went back to work, laying out Beattie's silverware on the dining table. Polishing the tarnish was normally a cheery business, working her way from the three-tiered cake stand to the English teapot and matching milk jug and sugar bowl, and then onto the napkin rings and Beattie's prized set of two dozen cake forks.

Not today, however.

It was pointless making the objects shine when they'd be scratched up again in a week. The repetition with the cleaning cloth left her wanting to pitch forward and lay her face on the table to sleep and never wake.

She forced herself to start on the forks with their fiddly tines. Beattie had told the story three times of how she'd bought them from the Theatre Royal Hotel when the owner, none other than the man who set up Tattersalls lottery, had demolished the popular pub to build a modern replacement.

It was clear in the telling that Beattie'd thought some luck might rub off on her, but Grace was of a different mind. Circumstance, not good fortune, was the force that either pulled you up in life or pulverised your dreams. And a cake fork was no use when you needed to dig yourself a quiet, deep hole and cover yourself with soil.

Grace squared her jaw and moved on to the teapot. Her tongue sought out the acid on her teeth and she was disappointed when the saliva washed the punishment away. She was absorbed in the effort of not thinking and didn't hear Beattie's shuffling step until she leaned in front of her. Grace jumped, and then did her best to pretend she hadn't.

'You've been working on that teapot for nearly half an hour. What's got into you, Gracie?'

Her voice was tender with concern, and when Grace could find no words to reply, Beattie reached out her hand and squeezed her shoulder. As she did, Grace exploded onto her feet, pushing back from the table and knocking over the bottle of silver cleaner.

'Sorry pet, I didn't mean to scare you. You don't seem yourself. Do you want to talk about it?'

'No, it's fine, I was miles away. Just need to keep my mind on the job.' The sentences came out flattened, through a face tight with the determination to hold back tears as she mopped up the spilt cleaner.

'You could do with some fun. Why don't you put on a frock and go to the dance on Saturday, meet some of the other girls from around here. You're always around us old ones and it'd do you good to make some friends.'

Grace's mind went to the blue dress still in its wrapping paper, a risky bundle under the bed. It could be a dangerous business going out in public with it clinging to her curves, drawing eyes towards her. She would never wear it. The thought of the dress and all the longing when she bought it was worse than Beattie's gentle touch. She made for the door before her wet cheeks gave her away.

'I'll talk to Greta, get her to let you finish an hour early so you'll have time to get ready.'

Grace paused, her back towards Beattie and hand on the open door, to nod her thanks. A mean pulsing began in her left temple and by the time she'd had a glass of water and tidied up the silverware, it was boxing the back of her eyeballs.

A couple of days later, Mrs Farley had clearly spoken with Beattie and was surprisingly positive about the dance, not because Grace might have some fun but as an opportunity for Teddy to be her companion. 'Do him good to practise his manners. He's going to need them next year.'

True to form, Mrs Farley didn't bother checking with Grace to see what she might want, or heaven forbid, if she even had an opinion on the matter.

Grace watched on as Mrs Farley spoke to Teddy about the dance arrangements, all the while floating as though she was up on the nearby shelf looking down. She saw a woman who was the hired help, chained to the magnitude of other's demands like the new pup to his kennel.

Teddy was already in his best shirt and pants, hair combed back, when Grace went to change her clothes on Saturday evening. She pulled her brown church dress over her head and straightened the sleeves, hurried a brush through her hair and tugged the strands back into a low bun, not bothering to pin the flyaway curls near her ears.

Earlier, at the table, she'd made an effort to chew the lamb chops and peas to mush. Her throat still constricted; however, sometimes when she swallowed it was only food and not a form of evil she wanted to eject. If she had to go to the hall and play the part then maybe she should at least enjoy the music, have a dance and forget the night of shadows.

Teddy's excitement boosted her mood and they chatted as they walked, dusk drawing in, easing them into a temporary intimacy. At the house, Lizzy usually occupied most of Grace's attention, but striding along the road she could focus for the first time on the boy. She sensed he was his own person, despite the demands of his parents and the farm.

'How are you feeling about going away next year?'

The boy was quiet for a time and Grace thought he'd decided not to answer.

'It's a good opportunity, you know; a chance to make something of myself.'

His silence, she realised, had been Teddy weighing up where she sat in the matter.

'Honestly, Teddy? I'm not your mum or dad you know, and this is between us. What do you really think?'

He jumped straight in. 'I wish I could stay and work on the farm, be with my friends. I don't wanna leave everything here and be stuck in a classroom with a pile of old books for another four years or more.'

'Have you told your dad?'

'No, and I don't want you to either. He's made up his mind we're going to have a lawyer in the family. I just wish it wasn't me.'

She patted his arm. A tawny frogmouth began a low groaning nearby, its mate answering in a soft rhythm. The moon was behind thin cloud, casting a ghostly blue light to show the way. Grace didn't try to placate the lad. It would have been cruel to do so; he'd already begun stretching himself into a future made by his family. They walked on and nothing more was said.

At the hall, the crowd was bigger than she'd expected. Members of the Young Men's Christian Association had stayed on after their annual picnic, swelling numbers. The teacher was on a low bench against the wall, talking with a group of mothers. On the opposite side of the room, the girl from the Post Office smoothed her hair and pretended not to be eyeing off the out-of-towners.

Grace had arrived empty-handed, and with a stab of guilt she saw other women entering with plates of cakes and sandwiches. Teddy slipped away to join a friend who followed them in with his mother.

Limp loops of paper streamers, pink, green and blue, were strung above the stage, and in each corner of the hall hung a kerosene lamp, the wicks turned up. Town councillor Ernie Calvert was calling the musicians to their instruments when Grace saw Beattie hugging three women clustered near the door before taking the nearest seat. She went over to her.

'Thought I'd make sure you came,' the older woman teased.

Teddy crossed the hall and kissed his aunt. As the pair of them chatted, Grace glanced around. The men greatly outnumbered the women, which meant she'd likely be dancing when her plan had been to watch from the sidelines.

Cr Calvert called them to attention and they all stood as the pianist thumped out the national anthem. The raucous rendition of 'God Save The Queen' picked up speed, led by the younger singers, and the pianist galloped along behind them, struggling to keep up. When it was over, Grace saw from the way they elbowed each other that they'd done it on purpose and she laughed at their cheekiness.

A foxtrot was called and as the ragtime tune began, a polite newcomer asked Grace to dance. Her mood had lightened with the laughter so she took to the floor, left hand on his upper arm, right hand in his but careful to avoid any other contact.

She was heavy-footed at first; however, led by the confident dancer, she settled into big-stepping and tight turns. Occasionally, he turned her out to spin. She'd never seen that with a foxtrot but she went with it, floating across the polished floor.

She accepted three more dances from the visitors and then sat a couple out. The night was more enjoyable than she'd expected, and after the supper break, she took a spot near the middle of the hall to watch the program highlight, a demonstration of the new Chicago swing dance.

The professionals, from the Pavilion dance hall in the city, leapt into it at full speed the first time, rapid steps forward, to the side, then two lock-steps and a stream of other moves Grace was struggling to follow. They travelled quickly down the hall and back, in perfect timing with each other, swinging hands out to separate with a one-handed wave then coming together, footwork precise.

The woman's patent leather shoes flashed as she moved, and Grace was mesmerised, studying the dancer as she flicked one foot elegantly behind the weight-bearing leg before swapping to the next, energy and excitement building in the dance.

It was a jolt when she lifted her eyes from the floor to see Clem's stocky frame against the opposite wall. He was looking in her direction while he yarned with a group of local labourers.

She scanned the crowd. Teddy was near the stage with his friends, but she couldn't see Beattie. The instinct to run was tempered by an overwhelming desire to hide under one of the benches, away from Clem's gaze.

The music stopped and the crowd pressed forward to watch as the dancers broke down the sequence into each round of steps. Grace shouldered her way to the wall. Her chest hurt. The few bites of supper she'd eaten were rising in a lump to the back of her throat. A lamp threw shadows across the swaying heads and shoulders of those gathered near, and it was hard to distinguish solid forms from the trick of the light.

It was the same rising, falling trick of light as the night she'd been on her way to bed.

She hadn't intended to walk into the darkness but the glow of the bonfire had drawn her across the paddock. She had never seen a fire like it, flames sputtering into darkness and a ring of heat driving back the cold. She had walked to the far side, partly to hide herself from view but also to keep the farmhouse in sight for the walk back. She pulled her cardigan tight across her chest and felt the heat pleasant on her face.

The night was still, the air suspended in the peaceful pause that came after daylight was released. The bonfire cast out warmth and smoke in a circle of calm. Grace felt her body relax into its frame, while the solitude emptied out her mind.

She smelled him before she saw him, though she had no time to make sense of what her nose was saying. He grabbed her from behind; he must have done because she lost her balance as he dragged her backwards, feet slipping on wet grass and her legs useless.

Then he was on top of her, a knee grinding into her chest, his hand jammed over her mouth and him hissing 'stay still or I'll kill you' while he fumbled with his pants. A few sharp stars shone above her in one small patch of night. She remembered it clearly, but everything else she flatly refused to let in, the sound of choking and the useless fight to stop the urge to swallow; laying on cold ground afterwards, a rag doll with sour mouth and matted hair …

She hadn't cried then but it was all she wanted to do now, cry and let loose a scream, but she knew if she let that go it would flood out, on and on, until there was nothing of her left. Instead she gripped one hand and dug a fingernail into the thin skin stretched across veins on the back of it. She wished she had a pin or scissors to open up a vein, gouge into the flow of blood, but at least the pain was settling her nerves.

As the demonstration ended and the crowd took to the floor, she looked to the exit but decided against it. She couldn't risk him following. A local lad asked for a dance but she shook her head and collapsed onto the seat, unable to muster any politeness. The look on his face said she was losing it. *Breathe. Wait for Teddy. Breathe.*

The final few dances stretched on. At last it was half past eleven, when a whistle sounded one long blast from the jetty and the young Christians collected their coats and left for the chartered steamer that had arrived to take them upriver. Cr Calvert thanked the band and the hall emptied out.

'What's the matter, Grace. You sick?' Teddy was leaning over her.

Torment was worse than a sickness, but she didn't want to distress him. 'I'm okay. A bit peaky, but I'll be fine after a good night's sleep.'

As they left the hall, Grace tucked Teddy's arm through hers, saying it was good practice for the time when he became someone's beau. She needed steadying and didn't want to be tempted to look over her shoulder the whole walk home.

SUNDAYS WERE HER day off and she sorely wanted to stay in bed, but she could do without the banging on the door or the raised eyebrows. She lurched to her feet and bent down for the dress flung on the floor several hours earlier. After breakfast, she piled onto the cart with the family and they headed to St Barnabas' for the morning service, collecting Beattie on the way.

Her mind whirred during the hymns and the sermon. The Reverend may as well have stood there mute for all she heard. Her eyes were stuck on the letters over the chancel, a useless, mocking sentiment. *Worship the Lord in the Beauty of Holiness.* The collection plate went around and she realised with a start that the hour was up.

Lizzy at some stage had bunched up under Grace's arm and she almost over-balanced when she stood up faster than the girl. They staggered for a moment in a tangle, causing Lizzy to dissolve in a fit of giggles.

The girl's merriment was too much for Grace. 'Tell your mum I'll walk back,' she said, hurrying out through the church porch before Lizzy could follow.

She followed the road in the direction of the lagoon

and took a rough track to the beach. The tide had turned and though the weather now offered more sunny days, the mountain summit in the distance still had a coating of snow. The wind sliced across the river, driving foam onto the sand.

She stood for a while, debating whether to walk around the rocks to the Pigeon Holes, maybe on to Opossum Bay and the end of the peninsula, or to turn for the township along the spreading curve of sand.

It was not a day for decisions. Without thinking, she began drifting along the beach in the direction of the jetty, past occasional boatsheds with rusting locks and sand piled up since summer, and the shacks where paint peeled on vertical boards.

The wide expanse of water and generous sky didn't fool her anymore. She was no freer than the moths in the jar hanging from Mrs Farley's apple tree, her feet stuck in molasses, so sticky that no amount of struggle would loosen them.

At least the moths had the hope of an opening where they might escape.

'Impossible' was a colour, she thought. It should be black but actually it was white — absorbing all colours but offering nothing of itself.

She could catch a ferry to the city and keep going. Run away down south, maybe get a job on an apple orchard in the Huon, or better yet, work as a maid in one of Hobart's fancy houses. She'd wear a white apron and a starched cap pinned to her hair and open a wide front door to greet important visitors.

Her as a maid, with grimy fingernails and calloused hands? Even the fantasy wouldn't hold.

What job could she get without a reference? If she took off without a letter, there was little hope of finding work and she'd end up in the poor house, a ragged nobody.

She was damned if she ran and cornered if she didn't.

It was hard to see any reason why she had life while Mary's innocent baby had none. The rescue home had fed her, clothed her, taught her to read, to say please and thanks and take orders that were plentifully given; yet never, not once, did they teach her that she mattered.

She was without mother, unloveable — for how else could her father forget he had a daughter — and the scale of her value was measured by a thousand tiny tasks finished every evening and every one of them needing to be done again the next day.

The wind had swung around to the northwest, and every now and then it blasted the back of her calves with dry sand. Hair was blowing over her eyes and when she pushed it back it was gritty, so she left it there. A pair of Pacific gulls rested near the edge of the water, bright orange beaks facing each other, and refused to move as she approached. She ran at them, flapping her arms, and frightened them into flight. It was satisfying to force them into the air.

At the top of the beach, she took the path to the guesthouse. As she entered the back door she was pleased to see Beattie's hat on the coat rack. The older woman was in the kitchen, two trays of biscuits on the table and a bowl of icing in her hand. If she was surprised to see Grace on her day off, she didn't show it.

'The melting moments weren't cool enough to ice before church, so the Reverend's missed out. Put the kettle on would you, Gracie.' Beattie slapped a blob of lemon icing on a biscuit and flattened it with a second one, placing the finished product on a tea towel before reaching for the next biscuit and loading more icing, working steadily to form even rows.

The rhythm of it soothed Grace and she began to relax. 'Who worked for you before me?' She hadn't planned to blurt it; however, now the question was out she was keen to know the answer.

'No one, love. With my feet getting bad and Greta having two kids still at home and cooking for the men, especially when the pickers come in, Rob and I got the idea of sharing someone.'

Beattie shot her a grin. 'It's worked out really well, I must say.'

The kettle whistled and Grace took the teapot down from the shelf and placed three scoops of tea in it. Her hand had largely healed, but out of habit she was careful to keep it out of the steam as she poured the water.

The two women settled at the table, cups of tea and a plate of biscuits in front of them.

'What about Jimmy and Clem? Have they been with the Farleys awhile?'

'Jimmy has, yes, been with them pretty much since the war. I knew him at school. A good sort. Help anyone out but keeps to himself. Don't think he saw himself as marriage material after he was injured.'

At Beattie's urging, Grace took a melting moment. The crumbly biscuit fell apart as she bit into it. She swallowed it quickly to clear her mouth for the real question. 'And Clem?'

'Don't know much about him. Not from around here. Think he showed up out of the blue around the time their eldest went timber-cutting. Looks like a strong fella.'

Grace didn't want Beattie to start asking questions about her sudden interest in the men because she wasn't sure she could handle it. She needed a question to steer the conversation away. 'You didn't ever marry, Beattie?'

It was the kind of thing you'd ask a friend, not your employer, and Grace braced herself, ready to be told to mind her business. Instead, the woman leaned in closer.

'I was almost wed, Gracie, a long time ago. We'd been sweethearts since school. He was a bit older than me and we'd planned to marry when I turned eighteen.'

Without noticing she was doing it, Grace ate a second biscuit. This was news to her. It had never crossed her mind that Beattie was once a young woman, just like her, with a future that included a husband and children.

'His father was a sea captain and he got a ketch to transport timber, twelve tonnes, a decent size. There was good money to be made carting timber, what with construction work around Hobart and off the island, especially in Melbourne. The *Mystery*, she was called. Vern went to work for his dad; it was his way to earn money so we could set ourselves up with our own place. He figured if he kept it up for a few years, we'd be right.'

The remainder of Grace's tea had cooled and she topped it up from the pot. She could see Beattie had arrived at a difficult place in the story and offered her more tea as an excuse to pause. They sat in silence for a few minutes, eyes on the table.

Then Beattie sighed and continued her story. 'Vern's older brother was working with them and they were on their way back from one of the big sawmills on the Tasman Peninsula, with a load of green timber and a nasty squall brewing at their back. It was late at night when they finished crossing the open ocean and came around the Iron Pot into the river. The older boy was at the wheel with only the mizzen and the jib set and no mainsail, 'cos of the wind. It'd been a long day and Vern and his dad were asleep in the cabin, getting some rest before she docked in Hobart where they'd unload the timber at first light. After the rough seas near Hope Beach, I reckon his brother thought they'd made it.'

This was more than a story, Grace thought. It was Beattie's life. The point where before met after. What happened next would set her on a completely different course. She wanted to hug the woman.

'The boat was near here, only a hundred yards or so offshore in Half Moon Bay. They reckon it was a wind bullet. You can see them coming in the daylight and do something, but he wouldn't have had a clue in the dark. She heeled over, taking in water real fast. The brother screamed out to warn the other two but they were stuck, the pressure of the water was jamming the cabin door shut.'

Grace couldn't help herself, she was crying now as Beattie explained how the brother did all he could. In the end, though, he had to save himself, taking the dinghy to raise the alarm. The next day, it took the Marine Board diver more than an hour to descend seventy feet into the darkest depths of the river so he could recover the bodies.

'I watched from the beach, though truth be told I don't really remember much,' she confided.

The diver had eventually burst through to the cabin and found the captain with his arms wrapped around his younger son.

Beattie was sad though calm.

Grace made an effort to pull herself together, before

asking, 'How did you go on, after him drowning right there off a beach you see every day?'

The older woman slowly got to her feet and began delicately placing biscuits into a large tin. She said nothing and Grace thought perhaps she didn't want to talk about it anymore. She pushed back her chair to leave.

'It's like this, Gracie. We get what we're given and that doesn't make it right, not by a long shot. But you can't change what is, and the true test of character is how you meet what's coming at you.'

Beattie's brother had given her a loan and she'd opened a small shop at the walkway to the jetty, selling cold drinks, newspapers, milk and a few staples to the shackies. Eventually, she'd saved a deposit for the guesthouse. Whether she'd decided not to marry another or the chance had not presented itself, she didn't say.

'The thing is, no matter what, you can still make a life worth living,' she said, snapping the lid onto the tin.

Grace turned the idea over, feeling the smoothness of it, a hard, white pebble she could hold onto.

She thanked Beattie for sharing her story, for the tea and the biscuits — after many difficult meals, she'd eaten three with embarrassing ease. She could see the woman was tired now and had aged in the course of the story. After washing up the cups, she left while Beattie settled into an armchair for a nap.

5

The strangled sound from the direction of the packing shed turned into yowling. Grace hadn't bothered putting the washing through the wringer a second time and it was heavy on the single line of rope as she battled to get the clothes prop under it to keep sheets and towels from staining on the loose grey soil.

By the time Grace had secured the laundry and headed towards the sound, it had built to a commotion.

As she rounded the corner of the shed, she saw the young border collie hanging by his neck, front legs scrabbling at emptiness, back legs frantically throwing up dirt, and Clem's hand through the dog's collar. On the ground between them was a chunk of ham from the sandwiches she'd made for the men that morning.

'You little bastard, I'll show you,' Clem was shouting, face flaming, as the pup squealed and yipped. He shook the dog and raised his free hand to thump him, but before he could, Jimmy grabbed his arm.

'That's enough, Clem,' he bellowed, 'he's only doing what he's meant to. Let him go for Chrissake.'

The pup was choking now, but Clem shook it one last time as if to let Jimmy know he hadn't won, and then he dropped him and the dog took off past Grace, tail down and whimpering, towards the house.

It was cowering near the porch when she got there, and when she bent to give it a pat it flinched and pulled away, flattening itself to squeeze under the house. She whispered to comfort it, 'It's okay, it's okay. Stay away from him, puppy, he's a bad man.'

Greta had heard the fuss and came out to see what was going on. When Grace told her how Clem had held the pup by the neck and given it a hard shake, all she said was, 'Well, it got what it deserved.'

A FORTNIGHT LATER, Mrs Farley told Grace she'd be away the next day, taking Teddy to town to sit a test for the grammar school to settle what class he'd be in. Her husband had left for Sandford on one of the horses the day before to help out for the rest of the week with his cousin's chaff-cutting team. The shortage of chaff and dry winter warranted an early harvest and, Grace gathered, the work would help tide the orchard over until the fruit was ready.

Next morning she was given her orders. 'Make sure Lizzy gets to school. She's going to play at Amy's after, then walk home with us. I want you to give the whole house a good sweep and dust while I'm gone. Get the rugs over the line and give them a good beating. Don't go spending all your time at Beattie's.'

If only, Grace thought. At least the work could be done without being under the hammer.

Jimmy had the dray hitched to take the pair to the ferry, but it was only when Greta and Teddy climbed up that she heard, with alarm, that Jimmy was going on from there across the Neck to work with the others on the chaff, leaving Clem to repair possum guards around tree trunks in the apricot grove.

As the dray turned onto the road she looked for Clem

and saw him pushing a barrow towards the edge of the orchard. *It's fine*, she thought, *I'll be gone to Beattie's before he's done.*

Bowls of eggs and canisters of flour and sugar were already laid out in the guesthouse kitchen when Grace arrived late morning. Beattie had a big weekend coming up, the Navalmen's Association annual cricket match at the sportsground, complete with a catering order for a big picnic lunch.

'Egg and bacon pies, sandwiches, sausage rolls and maybe a lemon slice and some jam tarts,' Beattie declared. They set to work making the slice and tarts, which would keep in tins until the big day.

Something had shifted for the two women since the day Beattie had talked about her loss, a new ease that sprang up between them despite the age difference. It seemed Grace had only been there an hour when the cuckoo clock chirped out three o'clock.

'Sorry Beattie, I need to go a bit early today. Mrs Farley wants me to have the dinner cooked by the time she gets home.' She washed her hands and threw her apron on the hook behind the door, Beattie's cheery 'bye bye' following her out.

She had left the corned beef soaking in brine and when she got back to the orchard, the first thing she did was get a bright fire burning before rinsing the grey froth off the large piece of beef. In went a bay leaf, onions and a few cloves, followed by chunks of carrot and swede to add flavour.

The pot took ages to come to a gentle simmer. She didn't want to risk bringing it to a hard boil and making the meat stringy, though when she did her sums she realised it might not be fully cooked by six o'clock. *Too bad, the old girl will have to wait.* She skimmed the bubbling surface a couple of times to remove the final scum and then went to retrieve the first of the rugs from the line.

It was heavy and awkward as she wrestled it into her arms, grumbling under her breath about the loose fibres that prickled her mouth and eyes. She shook the green paisley out on the floor in the parlour and went back to the line. She was at full stretch untangling the bedroom mat from the pegs when he grabbed her. She was still holding the corner of the rug as she went down.

It had been warm on the walk back from the guesthouse so she'd removed her cardigan and stripped off her woollen tights. As she hit the ground, the panic was pushed aside by the thought that she'd never get the black soil from her pale pink blouse. She clung to the thought. She might have screamed with the pain, she wasn't sure because she was already in retreat, to a small, dark circle in her head, a tiny dot of nothing, a full stop waiting to save her at the end of her only sentence.

It took no time at all, it seemed. She was back on her feet and must have been running, for how else could she explain the blur around her while she was as still as death.

She thought of the pup and the way it had cringed as it went into hiding under the house, but she was moving and there was no safe space. She must have fallen as she ran because her chest was raw and specks of gravel from the road dug into her hands. She didn't stop at the wetlands, couldn't stop, was not the one in control. She was a mass of arms and legs, pumping her through space until she hit the ocean beach. Her body lagged behind but she ignored its pull and propelled herself onwards to the waves rolling clean and clear, reaching to her, coming for her.

She slowed, but only a little as the wet skirt dragged, and she went to meet the blessed welcome of the sea. The surges were strong now, up to her chest. The water should have been cold but she didn't feel it. The sea rocked and roiled, pulling her shoulders under, then her head, until it had her in its full embrace.

Such relief, the weightlessness of it washing any resistance from her mind. Oblivion waiting, rising up.

She had the strange sense that here in the tumbling water she was not alone. She glimpsed a shape and flung out a hand to it but it was all the sea, waiting for her, wrapping around, holding her close. Its saltiness soft around her, taking her under with such care and grace, she felt no need to fight.

The bliss was taking over, oh such ecstasy she'd heard about in church but had thought it a lie from those who sought to keep good folk returning to the pews. It was white at first, her 'impossible' colour, then scattered into confetti falling in rainbow shades of blue, green, purple and gold. She was colour and rapture. It swayed through her, bending her to its play as wind might dance in a field of grain, and all around she felt a loving presence, sheltering, protecting, and any violence in the roaring water was of no concern.

She felt something jerk her and she pushed against its tugging but in the next moment the bliss was banished by rough yanking at her hair and a burning pain in her lungs.

Suddenly her mouth hit air and she gasped with the shock of it, the sky demanding that she breathe. She was flipped onto her back and saw Jimmy let go of her hair and grip her sleeve, grunting and straining as he dragged her to shallow water. By the time she hit sand she was coughing and spitting but couldn't stand. Jimmy fell on his knees beside her, where the final line of water broke down in clouds of sand.

A gull squawked nearby, but the loudest sounds above the surf were their ragged, heaving breaths.

'Jesus, Gracie, didn't you know there's a vicious bloody undertow here! I thought we were both goners.' He was trying to be mad but he was whacked and it came out in staccato bursts. He staggered to his feet but all she could do was get on her hands and knees to keep her nose out of the sandpaper scrub of the surf.

Her only thought was that the pot of corned beef had probably boiled dry. The absurdity of it overwhelmed her and she heard herself cackling, unable to stop even when Jimmy told her to get out of the water.

Eventually, he helped her up and she sat above the high water mark while he pulled the bottom of her skirt to one side and wrung out as much moisture as he could. 'I couldn't catch you up,' was all he could rasp, panting preventing him from saying anything further.

It was only when they'd gathered themselves up and reached the top of the dune that she learnt the chaff-cutter's steam engine had seized and Jimmy had been sent home early. He'd arrived to see her running through the orchard, he said, like Olympic legend William Hunt in the 220-yard dash.

'No need to explain, Grace, I'm sure you won't. But I fought in the blood and mud at Passchendaele and I can tell you now, I know what it looks like when a person's running from something.'

She didn't speak. There was no point.

An hour later, Grace had changed out of her wet clothes and was cutting vegetables at the kitchen table when Mrs Farley, Teddy and Lizzy returned. She wanted nothing more than to take to her bed and never rise again, but instead she mimicked vigour with the work to disguise the exhausted tremor in her hands.

Rob Farley returned home the next day. The problem with the chaff-cutting engine was more serious than expected and the work had been delayed. He, Jimmy and Clem had a day taking turns with the cultivator to keep the weeds down between the trees. She saw them late morning, having a smoke, as she left for Beattie's. It didn't matter where Clem was anymore. What did she care when she could no longer feel, when she was a ventriloquist's doll, doing the bidding of whoever pulled the levers.

At the guesthouse, Beattie knew something was wrong and tried again to get her to open up. Grace silenced her by leaving the room, not because she didn't trust her but because she didn't trust herself. If she dared open her mouth and let the words fly, they might turn into ravens and tear out her eyes.

She became a sleepwalker, drifting through her days, contained only by the responsibilities at the orchard and the guesthouse, and the thread of road that held the two places together.

She knew it was hard for Lizzy, who noticed the loss of warmth more keenly, and it seemed kinder in the end to tell the girl that those days were over and she was too busy for her childish chat.

She still went to church for the company of people sitting alongside her during the service, when no one would notice the absence of conversation. As for the dances that happened more frequently as summer closed in, Beattie made one last attempt to encourage her to go but gave up when she saw the girl would not be persuaded.

Not long after the incident on Hope Beach, Grace had gone outside to empty the tea slops when she heard heated voices by the bunkhouse. From the corner she saw Jimmy thrusting a fist in the air near Clem's chin. She didn't wait to see where the argument went but took the teapot inside, closing her mind to the two labourers.

Whatever had transpired did not amount to any limits on Clem. Quite the opposite. He grew bolder.

He bailed her up in broad daylight along the road, a mile from the farm, and tackled her to the ground under the eucalypt where the heron had once sat. Another time, when she thought Teddy was in the yard and it was safe to be outside, he shoved her against the back of the packing shed and pinned her where she stood.

It obviously pleased Greta Farley that Grace was more silent and willing to fit extra chores into the day, often washing up or working through until it was time to shut herself away in the lean-to. Grace figured the extra work would make her sleep but it wasn't the case. No matter how early her day began or how late it finished, she lay in bed for hours with a blistered mind begging for blankness to come so she could be released.

Christmas appeared and departed with little ceremony and extra work — she and Beattie did the three-course family lunch for them all — and 1925 slid in like a thief in the night. As the apricots ripened in January, it was busy at the orchard. When the pickers arrived, pitching their tents near the bunkhouse, Grace stayed in the house for much of the day to help with the extra cooking. In the daily frenzy of extra workers and deadlines to get the premium fruit packed into boxes, on the dray to the ferries and off to market in peak condition, Clem had no choice but to leave her alone.

Adding to the pressure of the operation, Mr Farley came into the kitchen early one morning and announced that 'some fool fisherman' had gotten cold the evening before and lit a fire on the timber jetty, causing considerable damage to the decking. Every available man was needed for hasty repairs to get it back in working order pronto. For several days afterwards the pickers kept going until dark to make up the lost time.

The next round of fruit picking was the late apricots for the jam factory in Hobart, and the men started at dawn to harvest as much fruit as they could before the day's heat kicked in.

Grace was preparing a batch of scones for their morning tea when Mrs Farley said she needed to talk to her. It was the school holidays and Lizzy was nearby, so the woman pulled Grace into the parlour.

This is it, thought Grace. *She knows it's not just the apricots ripening.*

For days now she had battled to do up her skirt, and the previous night she'd sneaked the sewing kit into her room to move the button across. Even with the adjustment it was tight. The moment had come. She would be homeless, just as she'd feared.

She stood tall just the same, imagining herself as a spinning top just before it slows and pauses, ready to fall.

Mrs Farley began a speech she'd clearly been mulling over for some time.

'I need you to do something important for me.'

Grace wobbled, with no clue about what the woman was asking.

'I'll be lucky to have the time to run a comb through my hair these next few weeks, it'll be so damn busy. I've been talking to Rob and he agrees it makes sense for you to take Teddy to Launceston to start college. He'll be living with Rob's brother and his wife and you could take him up on the train, make sure he's got what he needs, stay the night, and then come back the next day. I've been thinking he could go on his own, but he's a bit nervy about starting the new school and I want to make sure he gets there.'

Even in Grace's dulled state it had been easy to see that the boy's temper had been quick to flare lately. 'Won't Beattie be needing me?'

'It'll be through the week so there won't be as many shackies about, and besides, her lodgers have gone home for the holidays. Never you mind Beattie, my girl. I told her I'd let you do a couple of extra half days so she can get ahead before you go.'

As with all things with Mrs Farley, there was no room for debate.

6

Grace had never taken the train but she schooled herself to hide any nerves because Teddy was in a state. He'd cried after he left the house but she and Jimmy, shushing the horse down the road, had pretended not to notice.

As instructed, they caught a cab from the ferry to make sure the two of them and Teddy's heavy suitcase made it to the station on time, as there was only forty minutes to spare. Traffic was slow around the roundabout at the station and they had to wait an anxious few minutes before the driver could park.

Grace left Teddy with the luggage and rushed off to get tickets. The man behind the window reminded her they'd need to change at Western Junction for the Launceston line. By the time the boy's suitcase and her small bag were in the guard's van and they'd found their seat, the five-minute whistle was sounding.

She was disappointed at first because she'd hoped to treat herself to a cup of tea and a cake before they left but the novelty of travelling by train soon distracted her. She watched the river slide by on one side while on the other, Government House and the rear of the Botanical Gardens disappeared from view.

They were almost to the causeway at Bridgewater before she looked at Teddy. Her initial thought was that his troubled face wasn't her problem, but he was so downcast she couldn't keep her heart hardened to him.

'Tell you what, Teddy. You have the window seat and once we cross the river I'll go to the dining car and get us some barley sugars.'

By the time the train had started its steep climb from Rekuna, billowing dirty-looking steam, the boy was sucking on a lolly and looking a little brighter. Grace was feeling better, too, with each mile the train laid down between her and the orchard.

The trip was different to journeying on the ferry, which doggedly bobbed and veered as it made its way through the swell, always finding its way back to South Arm. Instead, the loco strained and clacked, marking out the distance in shudders and strange ticking sounds as it crossed joins in the rails or level crossings.

It was comforting to hear it towing her north, to know the rails set a path and she was on it to the end and all she had to do was stay in her seat. It wasn't about Launceston, because she didn't feel she was heading somewhere at all. No, she was in the business of leaving somewhere. It made all the difference.

At Rhyndaston, the train levelled out, and then the carriage plunged into darkness. It was Teddy who shouted, above the roar of the loco, that the tunnel they were in was nearly a mile long. Back in the daylight, they shared the thrill of it and began to talk about what else might come as they travelled.

After a companionable silence, she turned to address Teddy. 'You know, this might be a good thing for you in the end. Have you thought of that?'

He shook his head. He might be young but he was his mother's son and had some of her shrewdness. 'What do you mean?'

'You won't be tied to the orchard, doing your father's bidding, hemmed in by rain that doesn't turn up on time or jam factory prices, or work that leaves you too tired for family and gives no time for fun.'

The boy seemed interested so she pressed on. 'Once you're a lawyer you'll be earning your own money, setting your hours. Imagine, Teddy, you can travel if you want. Go to fascinating places. Live wherever it takes your fancy. Yes, you've got some years of study ahead but in the end you'll have your freedom.'

It was quite a speech and Teddy laughed as she wound up.

'Sounds like you're the one who should be getting a law degree!'

The mumbo jumbo of the legal profession didn't interest Grace and besides, being a woman put it out of reach, but freedom was another matter — yes that was worth having. She didn't need to pile on any pressure for Teddy, so she kept her mouth shut; however, the reality was that soon he'd be a man and forge his own life. He didn't know how lucky he was.

They ate their sandwiches and at one o'clock the train came to a halt and they changed for the branch line. As they steamed up to the platform in Launceston, she reminded him of the arrangement.

'I'll put you and your suitcase in a taxi to your uncle's and after I've done the shopping for your mother I'll follow on by bus. I have to leave first thing in the morning and the shops won't be open.' It was annoying that even on a trip to the opposite side of the island, Mrs Farley had given her a list, though it did have the benefit of giving her the afternoon in her own company.

A line of cabs waited outside the station and within

minutes, Teddy was on board one. She was so focused on making sure the driver knew the address she'd given him that the car had pulled away before she realised her bag was still on the ground beside her. She left it in a locker at the railway station and went looking for a café.

Over a pot of tea, she checked the list and the directions to Brisbane Street. Most of the purchases could be found at McKinlays, which Mrs Farley thought was far superior to any department store in Hobart. 'Quality, Grace. Their advertisements don't say "if it comes from McKinlays it's good" for no reason.' Grace checked her purse, marveling at seeing pound notes instead of coins.

She took a wrong turn but didn't realise it until she found herself near the river, which was flowing muddy and sluggish along its weedy banks. By the time she'd asked a pedestrian for help and found her way, the afternoon was getting on and she was in a hurry.

It wasn't seemly to run, though she was tempted, so she walked as swiftly as she could. With her eyes down and her thoughts a mile away, she didn't notice a man had begun to follow her and it was a shock when she rounded a corner, head raised to look for the street sign, and he charged her shoulder, knocking her to the ground and snatching her purse.

She'd fallen hard and lay winded, her mind frozen, the footpath pressing rough against her face and hands. Someone eased her up and asked if she was okay, but still she couldn't speak. An older man supported her elbow and led her slowly to a nearby tearoom, ordering two pots of their strongest brew, with no attempt to get her talking.

He was about the same age as Rob Farley, with streaks of silver hair above his ears. A working man, she thought, from the look of his broad hands and the way he seemed out of place among the small circular tables and the brightly white tablecloths.

The tea arrived and he poured her a cup, spooning in three sugars. 'Here, get that into you love, you've had a shock.'

She was shaking a little as she took the drink but its warmth as it went down was calming. The staff were busy, pencils on order pads, the kitchen door swinging back and forth, a woman ringing up sales on the till behind the counter, but the fellow was a still point in the bustle.

She had drunk most of her tea before he stirred and introduced himself. 'Alf Sturdy,' he offered.

He had been kind and she needed to make an effort to show she was grateful. 'I'm Grace, Grace Anderson. Here from Hobart on business for my employer. Thank you for helping me.' The thought of the stolen money was too much; she pushed it away and concentrated on the tea.

'Anderson, you say.' He had his head to one side, eyes scrunched, deepening the weathered lines radiating out from the corners to his temples. For a brief moment he looked at her in an odd way, like she'd just told him the sky wasn't blue but made from toffee. 'Where'd you grow up?'

It was easier to answer his question and wander away with words than face the trouble she was in — the sickening sense that it wasn't only the money; that all was lost.

'In Hobart. I grew up in an orphanage, was there from a baby, don't know much about where I really came from. My mother died and I never knew my father. Work on an orchard now.' The stream of talking was taking on a life of its own and she seemed unable to bring it to a halt.

'I also work part of the day at a guesthouse run by the farmer's sister so there's always plenty to do, what with all the cooking, cleaning, mending, looking after Lizzy and giving a hand outside.' She was thinking of how it felt every time she left the back door at the orchard and without meaning to, shuddered.

The tremor was nothing of itself but it set off a tiny vibration behind her eyes that rippled towards the back of her head. It loosened the wall of the dam she'd spent months making secure, and without meaning to, fat tears spilled over and she began to sob loudly.

The man shifted in his seat and she waited for him to stand and say his farewells now she'd embarrassed him but instead, he pulled a handkerchief from his pocket and handed it to her. It smelled of soap and tobacco. She blew her nose twice before she could clamp her throat to stop the rise of awful sounds that would have the power to empty the room.

'Doesn't look like it's a happy place, Grace Anderson.' His kindness made her want to cry all the more.

'I like working at the guesthouse with Beattie, but the orchard …' her voice petered out.

He ordered another pot of tea and two pasties. As they ate, he steered the conversation to his own work, at the pilot station at Low Head. He was the lighthouse superintendent, he said, though he showed no sign of particular pride in the title. He was a man of the sea and spent his time in sight of it or on it, and days like today, when he'd been required to attend a meeting of the Commonwealth Lighthouse Service, were a waste of good salt air.

He wasn't a conversationalist, that much was clear. The sentences came out stiff, sometimes banging one against the other or stopping suddenly for long silences when it seemed they should go on.

His wife, God bless her soul, had died four months back. They'd been married for years.

Never an easy life for a lightkeeper's wife.

They'd had babies but none had made it past childhood.

At that point, he ceased talking completely. Grace could see the grief haunting him, a sadness so complete it required no response from her so she gave none. The pasties were gone and she watched him chase a few crumbs of pastry around his plate as she fought the panic about the missing pound notes.

'Tell you what, if you're not happy down south, maybe you could come and work for me, cooking and cleaning. It'd take a load off, to be honest, and I'm done with finishing late and getting back to nothing for my tea. You'd have your own quarters, of course. There's about thirty of us all, what with the lighthouse, two leading lights on the river and the marine board's pilot boats coming and going to the ships. I'd pay you whatever you're getting now, maybe a few bob more because you'll need to cover rent, being as how you're not in the service.'

She must have looked stunned because he hurried to reassure her about the nature of the offer.

'The wives are there too, and a schoolroom for the kids, so it's not as if you'd be stuck for company.'

She pictured Beattie, shuffling out to the dining room with food for the lodgers, and the hurt on Lizzy's face when she'd pushed her away, and the whale lying dead on Hope Beach. Even as she had the thoughts, she heard herself say, 'That sounds grand. Can I start straight away?'

Such recklessness, she didn't know where it came from,

driving away the images of Teddy leaving in the cab, Jimmy panting on the beach, the fury that would be on Greta Farley's face because the purse had gone.

'I don't see why not, Grace.'

It was settled. He had a car and arranged to meet her at the train station in an hour. When he turned up, he gave her an advance on her first week's wages and pointed her towards the GPO to send a telegram letting Teddy's uncle know she'd found a new job and would not be staying.

'Don't want a search party out after you,' he said with a laugh.

Walking back to the car, she decided she'd write to Greta Farley at the first opportunity, a straightforward letter stating the simple fact of her never returning, reporting the theft of the purse and offering to repay the money when she could. It didn't matter what the letter said, the waspish woman would believe she'd stolen the pound notes.

To Beattie, she would express genuine regret about letting her down and thank her for the many kindnesses. She'd tell her to talk to Jimmy if she got the chance; assure her that he would understand.

Light rain was falling, washing the windscreen clean as they motored away from the station. Cruising up the Tamar River towards its mouth, something bothered Grace, an unfamiliar sensation. They'd been driving for half an hour before it made sense.

Out there, summer was preparing to depart but only now had her spring arrived. Blood was flowing again in her veins. She was so caught up in the deliciousness of it that she didn't think to ask herself any awkward questions, like why would a stranger take her in?

7

It was first light and she was balanced on the edge of the bed. She had no desire to stand. At the orchard one night, Lizzy had left her toy bear in the yard and a rat had chewed through the middle, dragging out stuffing to make a nest. When she'd picked up the mess the next day, the bear had folded in half.

Grace's body was now that bear.

She'd been woken by a mournful sound, piercing the thick layer of sleep pressed around her. The foghorn had blasted a second time and by the third, she had managed to struggle upright, disgusted to find she was still in her clothes and had slept on the bare mattress in the cottage provided by the Superintendent.

The enormity of what she'd done was inescapable. She'd fled, barreling blind like the day she'd thrown herself into the ocean. Well, she'd flung herself into something all right, and no one could save her this time.

The previous evening, they had made good time to George Town, 'originally the seat of government for northern Tasmania,' the Superintendent had said as they passed through.

She'd spied the tentacles of light pulsing from the tower long before they reached the end of the road, where a cluster of cottages and workshops emerged white against the gathering darkness. When the car had stopped, it had been an effort to get out. Despite not eating since the pasty, her stomach had churned and she'd longed to stay in the warmth and safety of the vehicle.

She'd been desperate in Launceston, not in her right mind. What she'd taken for opportunity now appeared foolhardy. She didn't know this man. She'd caught him looking sideways at her two or three times after they'd settled into the journey, his face expressionless. Or was it hiding something?

She was wrung out, couldn't tell anymore what anything meant. Angry that when they'd arrived, she hadn't thrown open the car door and bolted into the night. Then she remembered, her bag had been in the boot and it would have meant leaving behind what little she owned — the hairbrush she'd had since she was seven, a bar of Ivory soap still in its box, a face cloth, clean underwear, a nightgown, the blue dress.

'Here you go, Grace.' He'd opened the car door and gestured towards a conjoined cottage, separate from the row of doors and chimneys opposite at a terrace she would come to know as Pilot's Row. The one he pointed to was part of a pair of neat houses designed for boatmen and their families.

'Let's find you a bit of bread and cheese and get you settled in your place.'

It had been easier in the end to pull herself up by the door handle and follow him along the horseshoe arrangement of buildings.

It didn't matter how far she ran or how hard she shut her eyes, the make-believe she managed, and how much she hated her animal self. None of it mattered. Whatever she thought or did, she could not escape the reality that part of Clem was growing in her belly.

A loud rapping now made her jump. She dragged herself to the door and opened it halfway to find a lanky fellow with an open face, taller than her and maybe a couple of years older, axe in hand.

'I'm Tommy, and I reckon you'd be Grace,' was his introduction, firm but friendly.

She was still partly hidden by the door and didn't move.

'Mr Sturdy sent me over to cut you some wood.' He saw her draw back and made a quick assessment of the situation. 'Tell you what, how about I come back and get stuck into it while you're up at the Superintendent's. Okay if I stack it there?' he asked, waving a hand beside the step.

She nodded.

He pointed uphill to a house beside the tower, at the tip of the headland. 'That one's the Superintendent's'. Then he left.

Moving slowly, she went to a narrow table and filled an enamel basin with cold water from the tap. She took out the bar of soap, pearly white in her hand, its creamy loveliness smelling of purity. She held it to her face, rolling its curved edge down her cheek, and then forced the chiseled letters, stamped in the centre, against her forehead, pushing hard at first. When that didn't hurt, she began striking herself with the soap, battering the wide bone at her hairline. It was only the thought of turning up for work with a bruise that caused her to stop.

She covered the half-mile or so to the lighthouse at a brisk pace and let herself in to the Superintendent's place. It was four rooms, bigger than her two-bedroom cottage, and arranged in an 'L' shape with the front door sheltered from two directions. One rear wall had two windows that overlooked a grassy slope strewn with boulders. Beyond it, the ocean stretched to the horizon. The wall facing the river mouth was solid stone, affording no view from inside, as though the building itself was determined to avoid the constant watch over rocks and reefs at the entrance.

Smoke lingered from a pipe lit a while back and gone with its owner. The fire in the stove had burned low, leaving a handful of hot coals. A dirty frying pan crusted with egg had been abandoned on the hearth. Through the doorway she saw blankets knotted to one side in a wrought iron bed and a stool piled high with books. Nearby, clothes had been discarded on the floor.

The Superintendent had left a note on the mantelpiece. 'Morning Grace. Make a list of food, whatever you need, and do what you think fit. You can leave my tea on the stove, I'll be back for it around five.'

Well, she thought, at least he wasn't expecting her to stay and entertain him with chat while he ate.

She cut herself a slab of bread and lathered it with butter, piling it on so thick her teeth squeaked as she bit into it. Above the fireplace hung a cross-stitch in pale blues and pinks. It wasn't a street scene or a pair of bluebirds, the sort of thing she'd seen framed elsewhere, and she had to get up close, a mouth full of crust, before she could see it was three names in ornate, flowing letters picked out with painstaking precision. Elspeth. George. Madeline.

Here, in this room, had lived a woman who'd birthed three babies and buried them all. The careful handmade letters spelled out an intimacy that Grace was invading. She was an interloper in private space.

As she stared at the children's names, their mother's spirit seemed to rise and fill the cottage with the hope she'd had for new life and the hopelessness that dislodged it each time she'd been knocked to her knees. Her dream had died with her, Grace knew that from the woman's need to pin the babies to the wall, and it made her all the sadder.

She noticed, on the end of the mantel, a small crystal vase with three crumbling blooms. She tossed the dried petals outside. Near the laundry and outhouse, she found a garden where pansies, pink dianthus and sweet Williams jostled each other on the edge of a neglected vegetable patch. She filled the vase with all it would take — soft purple, yellow, maroon, and stiff red blooms — and placed it carefully under the cross-stitch.

The bedroom was pungent with the vinegary stench of an ageing man who cared little for taking a wash or making a fresh bed. She stripped the mattress and covered it with fresh bed linen from a shelf in the corner. Then she went out to the laundry and dumped the sheets and clothes in the copper. It was evident Mrs Sturdy had been well-organised; dry kindling was set for the fire and a bucket was at the ready to fill the copper.

While the water heated, she found a broom and began sweeping. She had left Hobart in her Sunday dress, so reluctantly, she took the apron from the hook on the front door, reasoning that Mrs Sturdy wouldn't have minded because the house was getting a tidy up.

A school bell rang in the distance and a gaggle of six or so tow-haired children raced past the window and downhill, elbowing each other and shouting. From the pilot station below came the sound of a hammer banging occasionally on metal, and in the pauses, she heard the steady, muffled *thunk*–pause–*thunk* of Tommy cutting wood.

All sounds were soon overtaken by the pulsing chug of the launch engine leaving its low-slung berth at Pilot's Bay. She went outside and watched briefly as it came into view and headed across the river. Then she got to work.

The rhythm in this new place was strange, jarring, unlike the orchard or the guesthouse, whose patterns she neither liked nor disliked but had made her days bearable with a scaffold of predictability.

She must look to toil if she wished to be saved from herself, she decided. It would be her sole deliverance because she could never ask for redemption, such a weighty word, dense with sin and evil, stuck together, sinew to bone. The prayer about straying from His Ways like lost sheep made it seem so innocent, that you created fault through a simple act of forgetfulness, an honest mistake in taking a wrong turn.

The ugliness of her sin could not be dismissed so easily, she was sure of it and just as certain that others would judge it as so. It was moral weakness made manifest, burrowing into flesh — a parasite and she the host. She dared not think about it, of the end when there'd be no more hiding the transgression, when it'd be exposed to the glare of the world. Never mind that it wasn't of her doing. It would take more than the perfect sacrifice of Christ Jesus our Lord and a few rounds of amen to clear away the blackening.

She had only one choice. Work was the path, the way to pay for what she'd done, letting him in, failing to defend herself from wickedness. She would slaughter herself with exhaustion and strive for reparation, but forgiveness was another matter because it could never come.

She started dusting the windowsill in each room and

then polished the mantelpiece, plumped the cushions in the two fireside chairs and scrubbed the table and floor. Yes, she thought, the work would keep her from collapse.

The washing had boiled in the suds and she hooked out each item with the length of dowel Mrs Sturdy had conveniently propped nearby. She gave everything a rinse then had to fight the mangle, as the rollers had been out of use for weeks and resisted attempts to turn the handle. Eventually it gave in and she wound the sheets, shirts, underwear and pants through twice. A sharp wind had sprung up from Bass Strait, and as she pegged the washing on the line, it flapped and snapped, a satisfying sign of order restored.

'Hellooo. Don't bother getting up.'

Grace was kneeling, digging up carrots, withered parsnips and a few thin-skinned potatoes when the woman stomped up.

A tall pole in green florals, she had a face long and narrow like a horse and big hands wedged on her hips. 'Mrs Jacques, the assistant keeper's wife.'

Grace stood anyway, turning up the corners of her mouth so it resembled a smile of sorts. After the exchange of a few sentences, it dawned on her that it was probably expected she invite the woman in for a pot of tea. It was a relief when Mrs Jacques said no thanks, she was only there to see if Grace needed anything.

'It's good you're here. I was so very pleased when Alf called in this morning to tell me and asked me to pop by.' She lifted her hands as if to make a gesture but they stalled in mid-air and she let them hang, useless. 'We felt so bad about what happened, a terrible, terrible thing.'

Grace's mind went to the cross-stitch inside. 'I see. Mrs Sturdy went suddenly then?'

'Mrs Sturdy? Oh no, she'd been ailing for a while. Awful business, her lungs so bad, wheezing and rattling through those last weeks, but at least she'd made it to sixty.'

The pair of them were apparently at odds, each standing in a singular stream of conversation without meeting in the middle. Grace had the distinct impression they were on about two different things, but the thought was swept aside when she saw Mrs Jacques cast her eyes down to the bulge beneath the apron. Instinctively, Grace scooped up the vegetables and clutched them to her waist, dirt and all.

'The postman takes shopping lists when he gets the mail Tuesdays, then the grocer's van brings the food and meat on the Thursday. Anything else you need to know, just ask. I'm in the place over there.' The woman waved towards the cottage on the other side of the tower and then took her leave.

The sun was bleeding its final rays over the river when Grace set a plate on the warm hearth with a few griddlecakes and pulled the pot of stew to the side of the stove. The meal was somewhat better than slop. She'd found a bacon bone in the meat safe in the laundry and the slow cooking with a little salt had drawn out the flavour, along with the vegetables. She'd already eaten a few spoonfuls and one of the griddlecakes, and had rinsed off her plate.

Back at her place, Tommy had left kindling piled alongside the larger chunks of wood and in no time she had a bright fire burning in her cottage and sheets on the bed. She didn't bother with the lamp but sat by the flames, letting them burn away the thorns of worry the fatigue hadn't rooted out.

The work had done the trick. She slid under the blankets and within minutes, sleep unhooked her body and she floated away, dreaming of a heartbeat against her back. She felt its steady pulse and in the half-light of the dream, she saw a pale figure emerge, with dark hair and no eyeballs, thunder rumbling in the sockets. Then the shadowy form dropped through a fissure in the earth, out of reach, endlessly falling.

THE WEEKS UNFOLDED and as they did, certain revelations came to bear.

First, that Mrs Jacques was a woman of action not idle words, keeping any counsel to herself and visits to a minimum.

She left a bundle of clothes on the doorstep, a loose shift, baggy wool jumper, a dark-blue skirt with a wide placket and row of buttons so a girl in Grace's condition could let the band out as need be. The clothes would not have fitted the rangy assistant keeper's wife, and Grace had no idea who'd donated them but she thanked Mrs Jacques, hoping all the while that any gossip would soon die down.

Second, there was no doubt Grace had landed in a place of industry and purpose.

The acetylene lantern demanded daily care atop the brick tower. The ships signaled for the pilot day and night and the men had no choice but to rev the launch and go, ignoring flood tides and stormy seas.

Less exciting was the endless task of repelling salt damage on cottage and workshop walls with thick coats of Berger's white paint. The tedium of returns to be filled, the fog record, night journal, day journal. Daily wind and weather reports called through to Melbourne on the one phone line. The ceaseless round of repairs in the workshops for the station buildings, the Tamar leading lights upriver at She-oak Point, and markers and buoys in the channel.

The activity, though, was tempered by a social pulse that flouted fancy gatherings and was instead found in a friendly nod or good morning. The loan of a few eggs or a spool of coloured thread. The way the men hoisted their share of unloading when the supply boat came in, the carpenter shoulder to shoulder with the senior assistant, the boatmen, coxswains and pilots in a line of sweat not rank.

Third, and this seemed most important, Low Head Pilot Station was a haven for misfits.

Grace had materialised from thin air and no one had blinked an eye. It had taken some nutting out but she was beginning to grasp that every soul here, except the children, had arrived in a similar way. Each one, like Grace, had a haunting at their heels.

It was visible in the way a man turned away from eye contact, a woman circled the need for questions. No one had history. A couple of the wives indicated they'd been here a while but that was all the background Grace got. It suited her to shelter in the balloon of being present, to shed the past. As for the future, that was like her impression of the heaving city of Melbourne on the other side of the Strait — unknown and best left blank.

Whatever the awkwardness on the night she'd travelled here, Alf Sturdy did not trouble her. They rarely crossed paths. He worked long days in the office adjacent to the head pilot, Captain Wickson. If he wasn't there, he was off in the car on urgent errands or filling in for shifts at the lighthouse or the leading lights when men fell ill or crisis took them away.

The brilliant white light that flashed from dusk until dawn, equal to a million candles, Tommy said, depended for its reliability on immediate repairs. The keepers had to stay on their game, with the all-too-frequent failure of temperamental gas mantles on the lantern, hourly hand-pumping of kerosene pressure tanks, and ships that turned up late or early signaling for the pilot.

If they were a man down for any reason, the Superintendent was usually the one to take the shift. He was boss of the lighthouse men — the Captain managed the others under separate jurisdiction — but Grace figured it was deliberate that he pushed himself when he could've made the younger men step up. Easier to stay away from an echoing bedroom and a set of tiny stitches sutured to a wall.

She was careful not to touch his wife's clothes, left hanging in the wardrobe with the one suit he wore to the monthly Launceston meetings, or disturb the little touches the dead woman had made in creating a home.

Grace left the silver-trimmed cruet set in its place except for lifting it up now and then to dust, setting it back in the same spot on the big dining table. The table and four thick-legged chairs had their own room, which the Superintendent never used, and marked out the respectability of the housewife they had served.

A sideboard displayed a sandwich plate, a figurine of a shepherd maid with a sheep, and a pair of oak candlesticks. She included the brass drip catchers and sconces in her polishing regime, first digging out the long-used wax stubs to fit fresh candles. A small trunk, leather straps worn thin on the edges where they'd rubbed, had been pushed under the table and left at an angle, an oddity in the formality of the room.

Occasionally, she shook out the rug in the second bedroom where a child's cot sat, empty, and a cradle did not rock, a frozen heart carved at its head. She gave all the care she could to the objects in the house, hoping to ease heartbreak drifting like dust motes in the air.

The only one at Low Head who was never fully occupied was Tommy, at least that's how it seemed to Grace, for he frequently came upon her in the grassy square between the houses or was at the door, seeking to fetch, to carry, or provide information she didn't require — a weather forecast, an update on shipping arrivals and departures, a headline from the newspaper. If he noticed her figure was blooming he said nothing, appearing to recognise, like the others, it was none of his business.

His reliable cheeriness was an irritation. He had a way of giving things a positive spin, of seeing the good in a person or a situation. The sailor in charge of the yacht that had run aground on Hebe Reef had done his best, was a victim of the sea mist and lack of wave action to indicate the rocks. The junior lightkeeper who spilled the oil had made an honest mistake when he opened the drum with the wrong tool. It'd been understandable that the schoolteacher, in her quarters behind the schoolroom, had gone to sleep by the fire and set her skirt alight when after all, she'd had a long day rounding up those unruly kids.

He often ended his sentences with 'that's the way it goes, it's just life'.

One time when he was at her door, more chipper than usual, she longed to swipe the happiness from his face and went to raise her hand before she caught herself. After that, she started looking out the window to see if he was around before she left her cottage or the Superintendent's house.

The first Sunday, her day off, she rose early out of habit. Daunted by the prospect of several empty hours, she left the cottage without bothering to have breakfast and took a walk across the promontory to East Beach.

As she pushed through the boobiallas and their fleshy leaves, a cloud of early mosquitos rose from the shade and circled around her, giving up the chase as she crossed grey, round pebbles lining the upper section of the beach.

Because the bay faced north into the Strait, the light fell golden on its long slick of sand and on the water gently lapping at the edge. Autumn hummed in the early morning coolness, plumping the air, softening sharp summer colours into deeper, mellow hues.

Grace had no plan and soon was lost in wandering and looking out for tiny shells, stepping carefully around a smattering of dainty flower patterns above the waterline where crabs had dug their breathing holes. By her reckoning, and all she had to go on was Mary's time and how her size compared now, she was close to five months gone.

She had the beach to herself and continued on, welcoming the peace, opening up to all the space. It settled her, gave her the chance to mull things over. She had made a home of sorts at the pilot station, more than she'd had in the lean-to at South Arm. No one watched over her shoulder as she did the work, and she'd found unexpected pockets of satisfaction in the empty dishes left by the Superintendent after she'd cooked a tasty pie or pudding.

As for the Low Head women, well, none of them showed her care like Beattie but they'd accepted her and that had its own kind of worth. She earned three pounds a week and paid seven shillings in rent so she was finally able to save. Best of all, she could go where she wanted without fear of a hand on her mouth or a punch for not laying still. She told herself there was much to be grateful for.

The rest of it she'd been able to keep at bay, in the newness of the people and the effort of the work. She hated the fact that the thing inside her, she refused to think of it as a baby, was getting stronger every day but the curve of her belly gave it away.

She began to step more lively, as though she could outpace the truth, but every step she took drew her closer to it. When she'd left the Salvation home, she'd been certain of finding freedom, a child feeding herself a useless mash of fairy story and foolery. She'd made mistakes and the worst had been to fill herself with the idea that she was somehow better than the sparse ground she'd grown in. Her time of reckoning had arrived.

She came to a halt near the top of the beach. What little she had in the cottage, the reliable job, would come to an end soon enough, and there would be a child with Clem's cruel face mewling for attention. There was no escaping it: her life was a mess, a bloody mess.

The certainty of it brought her undone and she sank onto the damp sand and wept. She whimpered at first and soon it built to a wail, for the mother who didn't stay, the boots that never came, the unloved ones lined up in their beds at the home, the aloneness yoked across her back. She let the tears run, mixing with snot, not caring that some of it made its way into her open mouth.

There was no holding back the slumbering grief, alive now, taking possession of bowels, stomach, lungs. She cried and keened for Mary, for the light that had gone from her eye, the wickedness that claimed her. For the loss of the only person Grace had truly loved. She moaned, throat raw, for the innocent little girl, for the fragile soul she'd held in her arms, soft baby cheeks, tiny hand curled around her thumb, and the silky, downy hair.

She sobbed, too, for the look on Lizzy's face when she spurned her, for what she'd crushed in the poor girl's heart. For ignoring Beattie's hidden pain, skating the surface of the woman's stories so she didn't have to give. And Jimmy, his damage far greater than any harm that could be seen, doing what he could to keep her safe even when it wasn't down to him. She cried for it all and for more she could never name.

The memory of Jimmy urging the horse on after the day in Hobart was a momentary comfort and she thought of him, smoking in the sun, the shorter leg causing him to tilt to one side as he leaned his back against the bunkhouse wall. Then into the picture came Clem.

Abruptly, she ceased the groaning and heaved herself to her feet, aware that the emptying out had not made her lighter but left her strangely heavy. Her body had become a cumbersome lump, an awkward walrus of a thing. She was glad when her sandy fingers accidentally rubbed grit into her eye. She could not, would not, cry for herself.

On the slow walk back, she caught sight of Tommy in the distance, motionless, looking out to sea. He turned his face towards her for what seemed an age but gave no sign of recognition, not even lifting a hand. She hoped he wouldn't come to meet her and was relieved when he broke away into the scrub and disappeared from view.

8

The Tamar River was deceptive. From the shore, as Grace walked each day between her cottage and the Superintendent's, she saw it wide and meandering. Its open mouth, though, was quick to suck in surging currents, while hidden rocks and shoals squeezed the navigation channel into a narrow bed that wound erratically from shore to shore. More than a few vessels had failed the test of Middle Bank, Whirlpool Rock, Porpoise Rock and other hazards.

While the lighthouse signaled the entrance to the river, the lead into the channel, just past Hebe Reef, was marked by the two lights on the riverbank south of the pilot station. When mariners lined them up, they knew their vessel was in position to enter the river. The significance of the Tamar leading lights was such that four men were stationed permanently at the site.

Hebe Reef itself was a rocky trap, right in the centre of the channel entrance and often invisible at high tide. It could break the back of a ship in minutes and had already claimed at least five vessels.

Captain Wickson was the kind of gnarled seadog the others called a veteran. As pilot-in-charge he led the crews, and it was his job to make the tricky transfer from the launch onto large ships to see them safely in and out of the river. He was called out about four times a week, sometimes more often or less, depending on the shipping schedule.

Grace took no interest in the origins or destination of the ships that headed to the deep-water port not far upriver, on the opposite shore at Beauty Point, or those that risked forty-one miles of treacherous shoals to the wharves in Launceston.

There was talk of the new port at Bell Bay, and men were being recruited for the pile driving operation to create the wharves, but it meant nothing to her and was part of a world she refused to acknowledge beyond the pilot station gate at the road.

She was planting out leeks behind the Superintendent's cottage when the incident began. Sarah Edwards, who spent more time in her garden than caring for her kids, had called by the day before with a parcel of the seedlings wrapped in wet newspaper. Grace had been thinking how she'd called her Mrs Edwards when she thanked her for the gift, but she secretly suspected the woman didn't have a marriage certificate.

The shouting came from the centre of the settlement and she hurried down to see several of the boatmen and tradesmen running to the jetty. In the river, opposite the bay below the pilot station, the station dinghy was making slow progress, and even from where she stood, Grace could see the men furiously working the oars.

Only twenty yards or so past them, something seemed to be going on with the cargo ship, the *Southern Star*. She appeared to be faltering and the dinghy made as if to get downwind of the bulky vessel. 'She's 6000 tons of trouble if they don't make a move soon,' Grace heard someone mutter.

The tide was running out strongly and the wind had freshened. Tommy had joined the group of onlookers. The launch was still at its moorings and she pointed to it, asking him, 'Why aren't they taking that out to get the captain?'

'The motor wouldn't work this morning when he was leaving. Dunno how they got him to Beauty Point, but he's a couple of hours late and they've got a helluva job getting him off in that tide.' She could hear the concern in Tommy's voice.

The dinghy lurched around to face the jetty and it seemed the oarsmen had decided to retreat. But as it swung towards them, the ship's whistle blew a long blast and the men stopped rowing momentarily, their small boat bouncing, before resuming their original course.

Grace and the others heard the engines grinding to force the vessel astern, but the tide had begun rushing out.

'It's tearing along, four miles an hour is my guess. They're not gonna make it,' one of the men said. As he spoke, the ship's stern swung to the west.

By now the dinghy was alongside; however, it was too dangerous for it to remain in that position and it soon cast off.

The gathered workers were running a commentary, voices betraying anxiety, but Grace wasn't sure who was saying what because she was fixed on the drama playing out in the river.

'He'll have to starboard the helm to beat that tide … yair, getting a bit close to Shear Rock beacon … Wickson's gonna need to get her into clear water bloody soon.'

The ship was coming round at half-speed.

'He don't need a big circle or she'll end up on the Dotterell Reef,' a man called Morgan said.

The panic in the men was palpable. The ship pulled away from the reef but by now it was eleven o'clock with a falling tide, and the current kept carrying her round.

The Superintendent had joined the throng and he was speaking with authority as though Captain Wickson could hear him. 'She's not going round fast enough. Christ, she's only in about ten fathoms there.'

As he said it, the vessel hit the end of Middle Bank and Grace marveled at how easily she ran aground, the tide pressing against her bow and forcing the stern further onto the submerged ledge.

Grace heard the engines roar at full speed ahead, and then after a minute or so, full speed astern but the ship didn't budge. They stood there for ten minutes or more but it was clear it wasn't going anywhere.

Tommy cursed and Grace got such a shock she spun around to be sure it was him. 'There'll be hell to pay for this. Twenty years or more, and Wickson's never made a wrong move but you watch, it won't matter a damn when they get him in court.'

'Now, Tommy, don't get ahead of yourself.' It was the Superintendent taking charge, even though, technically, he had no authority over the pilot operation. 'Davis, Morgan, you wait here and give 'em a hand tying up. They'll be buggered after that effort on the oars. The rest of you, there's plenty of work to be getting on with.'

The men scattered back to the workshops and the Superintendent went straight to his office.

He was already bracing himself for the endless phone calls and paperwork that would soon see him stuck fast, and at a desk no less, far longer than the *Southern Star* was likely to be on Middle Bank. It'd only be a matter of time and Master Warden Ritchie and the ship's agents would get wind of the grounding and be on their way from Launceston. While Wickson would take the heat, the Superintendent would be an important witness.

Grace also went back to work, finishing the planting and going on with her chores. After washing the cottage floors mid-afternoon, she walked down the road while she waited for the boards to dry. The tug, *Wybia*, had made its way from Launceston, and efforts were under way to get a line aboard the damaged vessel.

When she left for her cottage around half past five, she heard the *Southern Star*'s engines spring to life but there was no sign of it coming free, despite a rising tide. It was an hour later before she heard the engines again, and by the time she'd walked to the pier, the tug was towing the ship in the direction of Beauty Point.

Next morning, she opened the door of the Superintendent's cottage to discover his meal untouched beside a cold stove. She got the fire going and heated the plate of food over a pot of boiling water, covered it with a second plate, picked up a knife and fork and took the lot down to the office.

The Superintendent and the Captain had their backs to the door. They'd spread charts over every inch of the table and were bent over them in silence, as though any minute the lines and markings might rearrange themselves for a different outcome. They'd clearly been at it for hours.

'Sorry about the tea, Grace. I dozed off here last night and didn't make it home.' He went straight to the plate. 'I'm not one to knock back your food. Always good tucker.' He winked at the Captain, who also looked the worse for wear.

She left the pair to their discussions and went back to work.

Next day, a note was waiting on the mantelpiece. He'd be working late again and could she please drop off his meal on the way home. As the afternoon wore on, she decided it would be a pleasant surprise if she also took him a flask of hot tea.

She had no luck finding a vacuum flask in the kitchen cupboard where the crockery was stored and was set to abandon the idea when she thought of the sideboard. It was the obvious place to store a flask, given it was likely to be used so little.

Grace remained reluctant to rifle through Mrs Sturdy's belongings, but she reasoned it was for a good cause as she got on her knees and opened the matching wooden doors.

Behind the door on the left, a few tablecloths were stacked neatly on the upper shelf, with a wicker-sewing basket below. On the right was a large white soup tureen, which had a row of startingly blue cornflowers curling around the lip, the handle on the lid, and up the length of a matching china ladle.

The lower shelf had a collection of smaller items — a couple of vases, fancy glasses with long stems, a set of six pale porcelain cups and matching saucers. Her head almost touched her knees as she stretched down low to see all the way across the shelf. She was in luck, though; as against the backboard was a dark-green flask.

She lifted it carefully and slowly over the top of the glasses and chinaware until it was on her lap. As she steadied herself to rise, the trunk was at eye level. It was dented and scuffed, signs of the travels that had led it to land under the table.

On impulse, she dragged it towards her and unbuckled the straps. She didn't mean to pry and it wasn't as if it had been hidden or was kept locked. *Just a quick look,* she told herself. It was not her right to peer inside, she was moral enough to know that, but it wasn't as if she was breaching any trust. The trunk seemed out of place in Mrs Sturdy's tidy room and Grace was curious to know why.

As she lifted the lid, the smell of an old winter day escaped, stale and spent. Grace barely noticed; she was focused on what lay at the top of the trunk. It was a lace-trimmed christening dress, yellowing and spotted with age. Resting on the dress was a circular silver brooch with a pair of Scottish thistles in smoky orange Cairngorm stone. She'd never understand why anyone would celebrate a weed in such a way.

Grace lifted it out, feeling the weight of it in her hand. The brooch was similar to one worn by King George's wife. Grace had seen an old newspaper photo of it pinned to the Queen's coat when she'd been on an official visit to Edinburgh, inspecting sites bombed by German Zeppelins in the war.

Perhaps Mrs Sturdy also had worn it on a coat. It occurred to Grace that the thickness of the brooch was all that separated her from the touch of the dead woman. The thought made her feel a bit queasy so she placed it back in the trunk and closed the lid. There was more to explore and Grace was keen to find out what lay below the child's gown, but she shoved the trunk back anyway and reprimanded herself. It was not her place to go poking through Mrs Sturdy's life.

She made the flask of tea and got organised to leave.

The Superintendent was on his own at the office. Sheets of typewritten paper and bound documents covered every surface like the worry lines that bit deep in his face. He was distracted, so she set down the food and turned to go.

'Haven't had a chance to ask how things are going for you, Grace.'

She wasn't sure what he meant so she waited.

'You've been here some weeks now. The wives been looking out for you?'

'Thank you, Mr Sturdy, they've all been most kind.'

'Good, good.' He nodded, stuck for words.

A long silence followed before she bailed him out. 'Is it proving acceptable for you, Mr Sturdy? I'm happy to make any adjustments if required.' She hadn't intended to sound like a servant.

'Excellent, most excellent. No, nothing needing to be changed.'

Another silence ensued.

Perhaps, she thought, he wanted to raise the delicate subject of her pregnancy, and that was most certainly something she'd do her best to avoid.

'You've everything you need?'

The halting, somewhat painful conversation continued, and as it did it dawned on her that he was a man who saved his words for work and he had no intention of taking a private turn with their exchange. After several minutes he seemed satisfied that she'd settled in to life at the pilot station and she was able to leave.

As the date for the Court of Inquiry approached, Grace often dropped off the evening meal at the office with a flask of tea. The grounding had been a costly business and the *Southern Star* had eventually been towed to the repair dock in Melbourne by two tugs. A marine board diver had inspected the hull before it left and it was leaking in four holds. They'd had to unload the cargo of wool bound for

England. Someone would be made to pay.

Besides, the reputation of the pilot station was at stake, the Superintendent told her as much. The conversations were only ever brief and maybe that was why, but she sensed he was starting to open up with her.

He'd worked with Wickson for years and it'd been one error of judgment in all that time. And after all, the ship's master had agreed to the manoeuvre, that it was the only way to position the vessel in those conditions and get the pilot off before they reached the open sea. If not, the Captain would've had to stay on until the next port, which could have taken several days to reach.

The Marine Board was breathing down the Captain's neck — there was the matter of who would pay the costs if the shipping company sought damages — and the Superintendent was keen to do right by him.

'He's fortunate he's got you on his side,' Grace said.

9

She was making a cake next morning and had bent down to pick up the egg beater she'd dropped on the floor. At first, she thought she'd straightened up too quickly and pulled a muscle. She added a pinch of salt to the eggs, whisking them harder than necessary around the bowl until they were frothy. By the time they were ready for the sugar it had happened again, a weird tic or tightness in her abdomen. This time, it couldn't be ignored. It was a bump or tap, like the baby was knocking from inside.

She checked the recipe and pressed on, adding the caster sugar a little at a time, beating madly as she went. The cake was meant to be a treat. The Superintendent had mentioned how he'd loved his wife's jam sponge and Grace thought it might cheer him up a bit, what with the court hearing in two days.

She'd copied out Mrs Morgan's recipe. Davis Morgan's wife was chatty and inclined to get overly bossy about how things should be done in a house, but all the wives praised her cooking. Grace was pleased with the way she'd hatched the plan, swapping vegetables with Mrs Jacques for a jar of raspberry jam.

The oven was hot and the sandwich tin already greased and lightly dusted with flour. Grace had melted the butter earlier and mixed it with four tablespoons of milk and Mrs Morgan's secret ingredient, a little water to keep the cake light.

She continued whipping the mix, working up a sweat and watching for the point where it would look creamy. A rumble, like a bubble of wind, popped in the drum of her belly, near her navel, but she pretended she hadn't felt it and continued beating for a few more minutes, until it was time to add the flour.

This was the difficult part Mrs Morgan had said, and the cake would fail if Grace couldn't fold in the flour a little at a time while dribbling in the buttery liquid. 'Fold the flour in light and don't overmix it,' her mentor had warned.

Another bump near her belly button, firmer this time. Unnerved, Grace tipped the cup a little too vigorously and in went the whole of the flour, merging quickly with the wet ingredients. She grabbed a tablespoon and managed to scoop some dry flour off the top, angry at her own stupidity and so much more. There was no denying it was the quickening.

She didn't have another four eggs and couldn't waste what was in the bowl so was obliged to keep going. By the time she'd added the liquid and the remainder of the flour, she knew the finished effort would be a sorry sight. She poured it into the tin anyway and stuck it in the oven.

While the cake cooked, the fluttering in her belly continued. The heat coming off the stove was nothing compared to the anger burning through her, at the sponge that would be flat, the being that wouldn't leave her alone.

After fifteen minutes or so she yanked the cake from the oven. It had started to come away from the sides of the tin, the sign that it was ready. But when she touched it lightly in the centre, it did not spring back as Mrs Morgan had said it should.

She didn't bother turning the cake out onto the wire rack. It was all she could do not to smash it with her fist, and she left it cooling in its tin. It didn't deserve any more care than that. The cottage walls were crowding in. She had to get outside for some air.

She was striding past the rear of the schoolhouse when Tommy called out to her. He was up a ladder, pushing a ball of fencing wire into a gap under the eaves to block out the birds. 'In a bit of a hurry, aren't we? Everything okay?'

The question was innocent enough but she badly wanted to march on and ignore his incessant grin. However, she quelled the urge and slowed her pace. The pilot station wasn't a place for incivility. 'Just annoyed with myself for messing up some cooking,' she said. 'Everything I touch seems to be a disaster.' She hadn't meant to add the last bit and looked at the air in front of her mouth, hoping she might snatch the words back.

He didn't reply and she was relieved that perhaps he hadn't heard. So it was a surprise when he came down the ladder and stepped in front of her, though not too close.

He shook his head. 'Grace, you're a good woman. Don't you be saying that about yourself, it's not true.' His tone was earnest, kind.

It was too much; she feared the frozen field inside her might start thawing. She wasn't willing to risk it or to stand a minute longer in the warmth of his gaze. She turned abruptly on her heel and walked back the way she'd come, rationalising her rudeness as she marched back up the hill.

Best to give no encouragement when we could never be friends.

Next morning, when she barged through the door of the Superintendent's cottage, lost in thought as she recalled Tommy's attempt to console her, Alf Sturdy was standing there. He was freshly shaved and in his dark-grey suit pants, the jacket slung over a chair, though the sartorial effort was offset by egg he'd smeared onto the cuff of his pale-blue shirt.

'Off to Launceston shortly, Grace, special meeting with the marine board. I'll be staying the night to sit in on tomorrow's hearing, maybe even a second night, depending on how it goes.' He disappeared into the bedroom and returned with a small suitcase in one hand and in the other, his white shirt and striped tie on a coathanger.

The nugget and shoe brushes were already on a sheet of newspaper laid out on the table and she went to them, polishing his dress shoes while he filled his tobacco pouch.

'By the way, thanks for the cake. You can see I enjoyed it.'

A crumb-coated knife was beside the cake, which was missing a large chunk. She'd managed to cut the flop in half and fill it with a thick layer of jam, at the last minute covering it with lemon icing so it could pass as a butter cake rather than mock what a sponge should be.

She put it back in the cupboard while the Superintendent busied himself to leave.

His departure was a problem for Grace because it meant no evening meal to cook, and the washing up and cleaning she did today would not be in need of redoing tomorrow. The prospect of all the spare time was a bother.

A few hours later, after letting the stove go out so she could give it a coat of black lead, she was pleased to have a solution. She would finish up here and then go to the schoolteacher and offer assistance for a half-day tomorrow. Surely the classroom could do with a clean.

Sleep was elusive that night, no matter how hard she

longed for it to come to the bed and cover her with its cloak of nothingness. Yesterday's gentle bumping near her navel had shifted lower, and the loathsome thing was now more insistent, shoving against her bladder. She pulled on the baggy jumper and made a dash for the outhouse.

Back under the blankets she debated which was more detestable, the creature growing inside her or the body that was allowing it to happen.

She'd almost convinced herself it wouldn't get this far, that the complex process of cells dividing, forming skin, fingers and toes, ears and eyelids, organs and bone, would collapse on itself, any minute grinding the sperm-driven growth into bloodied pulp her body could expel. If only it was a tumour, an unwanted mass waiting for a surgeon to cut it out with a blade.

The night wore on and eventually the movement stopped and she could, at last, escape to sleep.

THE TEACHER WAS delighted to discover that Grace could read and write and immediately dismissed all suggestion of cleaning. Instead, she set her to work the next afternoon, helping two of the younger girls with their spelling and writing.

Miss Munro was in her first posting after teacher training college and unlike the classroom Grace had known, refused to reign over the twelve children with terror.

The schoolmistress didn't box the children's ears or smack their faces to keep them in line. During the afternoon break, she confided in Grace that she didn't aim to be their friend either. She issued instructions with a firm authority and understood that detentions keeping them from outdoor play in the lunch break or after school were punishment enough.

Grace's two charges, Ruby and Connie, were excited to have a visitor help with their Grade Two spelling books, jostling to see who could sit closest as she encouraged them to sound out the words highlighted on each page. At the end of each word list, she got them to turn over their books and dictated one word at a time for them to practise writing.

Despite her best intentions, Grace found herself warming to their childish joy and the way they curled their hands to push the thick, black pencils across the page. She knew nothing about Connie or her family, who lived at the far end of the square in the coxswain's cottage, but sunny little Ruby was a different matter.

This was a maritime community and for all its regulations and systems, it lived by the rule of the sea and the river. Ruby's family understood that more than most.

The girl had an older brother who'd drowned a few years earlier, knocked unconscious when the boom flipped on the small dinghy he and two friends had been learning to sail. He had been dead weight when he hit the water and hadn't stood a chance. His remains, they said, had been terribly disfigured by the fish.

The afternoon passed quickly with only one disturbance, when the Jacques' older boy attempted to argue with Miss Munro about the value of learning geography when he'd likely end up working on a building site in town.

At half past three, the children put their chairs on the desks and Grace swept the floor while Miss Munro washed down the blackboard, closed the windows and sharpened pencils for the marking she'd do after tea.

She was quick to thank Grace as she left. 'You're welcome back any time. You're a natural with the children.'

The praise was unexpected and Grace brushed it off; however, she had to admit, she'd enjoyed her afternoon.

The Superintendent must have driven in late because he was back next morning.

Grace passed him on the way up the path. It wasn't her place to ask but she couldn't help herself. 'How was it?'

He propped alongside her. 'The Captain took all the blame. Bloody fool. I told him not to, just to give the full facts and let the ship's master do the same and see where the cards fell.'

It was a lot of information and he was still winding up. 'Even Meredith, the board's secretary, gave evidence they'd never provided any written instructions about a pilot leaving a vessel in rough water. Whether through what they did or didn't do, they all had a share in what went wrong. But the Captain let 'em hang him out to dry.'

They parted ways, the Superintendent grim as he headed to his office.

A few weeks later, the verdict came in. Grace read the newspaper the Superintendent had tossed on the floor by his stove. A Police Magistrate had led the inquiry team, which included two captains who served as nautical assessors.

In the opinion of the court, the casualty was due solely to the pilot's error of judgment in putting the engines astern in the strong ebb tide, causing the vessel to swing across the channel into a dangerous position.

Wickson had already resigned, handing in his letter the day before the findings were released. Within the month, his wife Louisa would become poorly and die at their new Launceston home, leaving him without job or comfort.

It seemed to Grace that life wore you down with endless grit. Every passing day, the world became a sadder place. Yet the baby filling her uterus remained determined to come into it.

10

By the end of March, Grace was a sleepwalker in her days and thanks to her passenger, as she'd come to call it, an insomniac in the long, chilly nights. Whatever heat once fanned her spirit had cooled to a low fire, dying a little more as each midnight rolled by.

She was more than six months, each week taking her closer to the birth she hadn't chosen and further from any prospects beyond that point. The worry about what she might do was endlessly circling in her head. Whatever route her thoughts took, winding through thickets of what could have been done differently or not at all, they always zigzagged to the same dead end.

She didn't want to give birth at all; however, it was too late for that option. She could dump the baby at the door of an orphanage but that would leave it to the same fate as her. Maybe adoption, then; give the obstinate thing away to a loving couple. But could she cope afterwards with the knowledge she'd left a cuckoo in their nest?

An alternative was both more permanent and disturbing. The woman of scruples she'd once thought herself to be had begun to fantasise about hiding away for the birth and then smothering the result.

In the lurid details — the pillow, the lack of struggle, what little effort would be needed to snuff out such a small life — she knew herself capable of the act. She walked backwards to meet Mary again, except her one-time friend wore the face of her own violent self. The image of a baby's crushed features was hideous, but worse, much worse, was the certainty of what she'd discovered in her own twisted heart.

The pressure of what to do was consuming her, so it was a jolt when a letter arrived from her previous life. When she tore it open and found it was from Beattie, she expected to feel some excitement; however, other than the recognition that she had a past, she felt nothing. Beattie had probably penned it at the big kitchen table, warmed by a stripe of morning sun.

It hasn't been the same since you left.

The letter was short, the pattern of indentations in the paper suggesting Beattie had made an earlier draft or two before writing the version she'd posted. She'd been stunned when Grace failed to return, and a little hurt, because there'd been no attempt to talk to her about any plan.

At that point, the tone of the letter turned. Grace knew Beattie loathed cricket, but the older woman wrote she'd seen Jimmy on his way to the sportsground one Saturday afternoon and on impulse had hobbled over to the game.

I wish you'd been able to tell me. It must have been terrible, Gracie. I'm so, so sorry. Evidently Jimmy had a word with Rob the day you left and my brother sacked Clem on the spot.

He'd have been gone from the orchard while she was still rocking on the train with Teddy.

It should have made her feel better that Clem got his comeuppance or that Beattie, so kind to Grace, knew why she ran or at least some of it, but the longer she stood there with the letter in her hand, the more disgraced she felt. She was sullied, dirty in the way that no amount of bathing could ever wash clean.

Clearly no one at South Arm knew about the pregnancy.

If you could see your way to coming back, I would be glad to put you up here and give you work. If not, I understand and hope you'll stay in touch.

The ending was the truly awful bit of the letter.

You're a good person, Gracie, and you deserve happiness and love.

Beattie could not be wider from the mark. A wise, astute woman, she'd failed to see that Grace warranted not a jot of either.

Mrs Jacques was knocking at the door. Grace threw the letter into the fire and watched it burn before she let her visitor in. The woman was calling more frequently than ever. For a competent housewife, managing three lads and two young girls, she seemed to be forever asking to borrow one ingredient or another that she'd found was running low.

It was odd because Mrs Jacques was a lighthouse woman, a different breed to the wives of the boatmen and others who worked for the pilot station. She observed the lighthouse creed — 'don't be dropping in whenever you like, mind your own business and let others take care of theirs'.

Grace was tempted to ask her if she needed help drawing up her shopping list. Fortunately, before she got so bold as to make the suggestion, she twigged to what was going on. The woman, in her own way, was keeping tabs on her. After that, Grace was careful to show a bit more cheer in her interactions with Mrs Jacques or anyone else, for that matter.

Tommy, too, was keeping an eye on her, but he exhibited it the opposite way to Mrs Jacques. Where she turned up to borrow, he turned up to give. He'd made Grace a wooden bread bin, which had necessitated a follow-up visit to give her the beeswax to polish the timber and a further opportunity to drop by with a specially turned knob he attached to the lid.

She saw it all passing by at a clip. It was happening behind the same pane of glass that had sheltered her that day at the Palace Theatre while a rowdy bunch of sailors corralled her in the foyer like she was a helpless sheep.

Occasionally, since she'd helped at the school, Miss Munro would call her into the schoolroom for a chat at the end of the day. The young teacher was the only other unmarried woman at the pilot station and Grace could see she was lonely. The teacher didn't force conversation onto Grace, so she was happy to oblige by providing some company when invited. Soon they were on first name terms.

It was Lillian Munro who asked what nobody else could. 'What will you do, Grace? When the baby comes.'

Out in the open, as it was, the question was brazen, even a little brash. Grace knew the teacher meant no harm, was asking from concern, but it was a question she'd been defending herself against for six months. The query had been made so easily but the answer was impossibly hard.

'I don't know. I haven't decided yet.' It was the best she could do, and even to her ears it sounded pathetic. Soon after, she bid farewell to Lillian and scuttled home.

Through the night and into the day, the teacher's question tormented her, running on a loop, unrelenting. If it had been an old boot, she'd have kicked it off; however, it was caught in her mind and not so easy to dislodge.

Overcome by the weariness of it, she had finished work and was nearing her cottage when she caught sight of Ruby playing at the end of the pier. She was on her own, a slight figure absorbed in scrambling and leaping on the edge of the pile of rubble that formed the base of the jetty. Grace smiled at the girl's evident pleasure in her game and looked away for a moment.

When she glanced back, Ruby had disappeared.

She looked towards the other houses and up the path to the lighthouse, but all was quiet. No sign of Ruby.

A sick feeling drew her to the pier and she ran its length. The river was high and spilling out towards the sea, the current strong. The dying sun threw dark, shifting shapes onto the surface. A blacker patch caught Grace's eye and she recognised Ruby's hair and then saw one pale hand slip from sight.

She kicked off her boots, or did she? She called for help, or maybe forgot to? By the time she broke the water, she was impelled by a kind of madness that killed all thinking, every impulse trained on the spot where the girl floated, one arm now flailing.

The tide carried Grace along, and despite the weight of her skirt she was kicking hard, pulling through the water with a steady stroke like she could never manage in surf, and soon she was gaining on the girl.

She reached her and with one lunge managed to grab a handful of the hair, jerking Ruby up and jamming a hand under her chin. The child was still. Grace began towing her towards the riverbank, swimming clumsily with one hand. She knew enough of the river not to cut across the current and aimed for a gradual line towards the land as it carried them both downstream. She heard Ruby choke, gulp in a mouthful of water and choke again. She had no breath to even say the girl's name.

It may have been minutes or an hour, she couldn't tell, but she was near to losing her grip on the girl when her foot got purchase on a rock, then another, and she was pushing Ruby forward into shallower water and a welcoming pair of hands waiting to receive the child.

She had no sense of how far they'd come from the jetty or how fast, or who it was that helped deliver the girl onto solid ground.

What she did remember, so clearly, were arms pulling the limp child away and as she went, the awful weight of her own wet bulk bearing down. Then, without a thought, as natural as the moon rising up when the sun left the sky, her body turning away, returning her to the buoyancy of the river and its certain course to the sea.

As she pushed back into the river she knew, absolutely, the water would save her. No matter that Satan's spawn was within, she'd be welcomed, whole, into the arms of the sea. The current hooked her and she went effortlessly into its stream.

Any agonising done on land could never deliver answers because the earth held none. It was so clear now, the sea was where she belonged, and the river would take her home. Not for a second did she think that she'd chosen the way to dying, to the lightless void where not a single star shone. No, Grace Anderson was not travelling to her end but going the other way at last, gladly, willingly, to her source.

She swam for as long as she could and when she could no longer swing her arms, she struggled, she couldn't say for how long or how much, out of habit not necessity. The river plucked at her clothes, pulling her head under and then playing her out so she bobbed to the surface again. The next time, it kept her down until her lungs were on fire, but still she was not afraid. When she burst momentarily through the surface, her body breathed from instinct as it found air.

When she sank the third time, she knew her lungs wouldn't fill with oxygen again and waited for the burning to pass. The pain retreated and flooding into its absence came a peace she'd never known — emptiness, gloriously, wonderfully holding nothing and yet full and complete.

Her body floated lightly, unbound, unencumbered. She no longer saw shape, colour or form, only the soothing jewel-red of blood or wine in the chalice cup. The river was bleeding and it was a thing of beauty.

Like the day in the surf at South Arm, the water cocooned her, embraced her. She and the water, its presence, were one and any fight to strive or decide or survive were done. Her life had been shaped by absences, stacking tight one after another and now, it no longer mattered. The baby no longer mattered. She no longer mattered.

The water carrying her along was her liberation, containing everything. She sensed it through her skin, all that it knew, a truth so pure and immediate, without a need for words. She'd tried so hard to fashion a woman from all the disconnected and missing parts, the buried pain, and it was never going to work. She understood, at last, as she let the water hold her.

A dull roaring was all around and it seemed her senses were reaching a peak, one single symphony of merging sound, sight, sensations in an effortless flow, all water, boundaries blurring. She hoped she'd reached the soft salt of the sea.

But no, she was still in the river, she must be because she'd snagged. Something caught her under one armpit and then two, bringing her violently to a halt. She tried to shove it away, to prevent it forcing her against the flow. The urge was strong to fight but her limbs had long since worn out and would not obey. It was only as she was dragged clear, in the brief moment before she lost consciousness, legs slapping against the ladder of the boat, that she recognised the sound had been the engines of the pilot launch.

She was awake long before she summoned the will to open her eyes and when she did, it was dawn. She was in her bed, an aching, beaten wretch.

Mrs Jacques was dozing nearby in a chair. She'd told the other women she'd step in, for if Mrs Sturdy had been alive she'd have kept watch and Mrs Jacques was the obvious one to fill her place. The truth was, in fact, that she wanted to be there.

At the sight of Grace's eyelids flickering open, she came and sat on the edge of the bed, reaching out a hand to stroke her hair, an unexpectedly tender voice emerging from her bony frame. 'How're you feeling, Grace? You've had a terrible time.' She didn't seem to expect an answer and Grace gave none, save for a small tilt of her chin. 'I'll warm up the chicken soup. You need to build your strength, the doctor's very worried about you.'

Grace was dozing when Mrs Jacques returned carrying a bowl and a plate with a thick slice of bread. 'I wasn't sure if you'd prefer toast, but I can soon fix it if you do.'

Grace accepted the woman's help to prop herself up on pillows. Her muscles were pounding, pellets of pain exploding under the skin with every move. Once she got upright she remained very still, unwilling to set it off again by drawing the spoon to her mouth.

Mrs Jacques made no comment but took the bowl and began feeding Grace with such calm intent that Grace felt no need to resist, opening her mouth for each spoonful of soup. She was no innocent, no baby bird needing care, but she accepted the food just the same.

Afterwards, she drifted into a twilight zone for hours, hearing an occasional knock at the door and Mrs Jacques turning away each caller with a quiet message that there would be no visitors today.

When she woke fully, the doctor from George Town had arrived and he asked to speak to Grace alone. Mrs Jacques took his jacket and closed the door behind her.

Doctor Grey had many working years behind him and few ahead. His straining braces held pleated pants stretched tight across a spreading waist, proof that he had a good appetite for food and drink; while a well-clipped moustache showed a man who took care of his appearance. 'How are you today, young Grace? You look much better than you did last night.' He smelled of harsh astringent and boiled lollies.

'I'm okay. How's Ruby though, is she recovered?'

'She's perfectly fine. I've just been to see her and she's up and running around. You're a very brave woman, saving her like that. There's a lot of people wanting to thank you when the time is right.' He pulled the chair closer and lowered his voice. 'I examined you thoroughly last night.

You're seven months, give or take a week. I don't know how you got that girl to shore.'

Grace didn't know either, her memory of events wiped clear, at least for now, by exhaustion.

'The thing is, Grace, the Superintendent had a word with me this morning.'

She badly wanted to change position, to get more upright so she could bear the load of what he'd been charged to say, Alf Sturdy not even wanting to deliver the news himself — that she should pack her bag, it was time for her and the bastard baby-to-be to take their leave from Low Head.

She must have begun crying because the doctor was shushing and saying that there was no need for tears.

'When you were being swept down the river, one of the assistants was leaving the lighthouse to take his turn at going for tea. He saw you battling your way to shore with the girl and he was the one who clambered out across the rocks and took the child from you.'

The doctor paused, as in the other room Mrs Jacques opened the oven door and slammed it shut. Grace heard Miss Munro ring the bell to call her pupils back to their desks for afternoon lessons.

'He saw what you did, Grace.'

She was confused now, the doctor was making no sense and she wondered briefly if perhaps he was too old for the job.

'He told Mr Sturdy last night, what he saw. That in all the commotion, with men running up the river and shouting, and the girl collapsed in his arms, it was plain you had your feet on solid ground. That you went back out into the river, deliberate like.'

Doctor Grey was trained in asking questions and making observations in the privileged bond between medico and patient. He stayed for more than an hour, during which time he had much to say while Grace could only give an occasional answer and try to take it in.

Other doctors might settle for treating the infection but, in his humble opinion, based on four decades of experience, it was always better to dig around and remove the splinter.

So it was that, supported by the leisurely cushion of his visit, Grace let her story spill out. He accepted it without challenge or judgement, every part, including Clem and the revulsion for what he'd left inside her. As she reached the end, she began lapsing into slumber that would stretch through the night and into much of the next day. The last thing she heard was the doctor speak quietly for a few moments as he collected his coat from Mrs Jacques, on the way out.

He returned the following afternoon, entering Grace's bedroom accompanied by Mrs Jacques. He checked his patient's vital signs and then cleared his throat. 'You're stronger today, Grace, but the only way you're truly going to get well will be when things are decided about the baby.'

Mrs Jacques nodded as he spoke, chiming in, 'I've been wanting to discuss it for some time and I feel bad it never seemed right to push you about it before.'

Grace had no idea the woman had felt that way. 'Mrs Jacques, I ——' she began but was swiftly interrupted.

'Call me Joyce, it's high time you did.'

The doctor outlined the plan. When Grace got close to her confinement, she would go to the six-bed midwifery home at George Town and await the birth. She did not have to decide what would happen to the child until afterwards, and the nurse in charge could give her advice.

Joyce spoke up, saying, 'Mr Sturdy's made it most clear that no matter your choice, you must return to your cottage and if you wish, continue with your work. He's never seen it any other way.'

With that, they left Grace to dress for the first time in three days so she could join them at the table for a slice of fried beef with bubble and squeak. Afterwards, the doctor went on his rounds and Joyce went home to attend to some chores, declaring Grace well enough to see to the fire in her absence.

The woman returned mid-afternoon with a plate of scones, apricot jam and whipped cream. 'Thought a treat wouldn't go astray.'

Grace bit into one scone out of politeness, but the jam brought her tastebuds alive and she soon moved onto a second one. They ate companionably over steaming cups of tea.

'You know, Grace, it's not the wee one's fault.' Joyce let the words hang in the air for a while. Getting no response she ploughed on. 'The sins of the fathers are not visited on the sons, or the daughters for that matter. If they were, none of us could get out of bed in the mornings.' With that, she gave a full-throated laugh.

10

Word had gotten out on the Friday that Grace was home alone, no longer needing Joyce's care. Ruby was the first to knock, accompanied by her mother and carrying a five-pound bag of chocolates and a handmade card.

The Superintendent arrived late morning, knocking his pipe on the step before entering the cottage. He declined the offer of a brew but she insisted, so he took a seat at the table. 'Good to see you up and about. You gave us a right scare, you know.'

While they waited for the kettle to boil he spoke about the loss of the Captain and how it had hit the boat crews hard; however, the marine board would advertise for a new head pilot at the weekend. 'Expect I'll be on the panel for the interviews,' he mused.

It was a short visit, just long enough to drink his tea and work up to what he'd really come to say. 'I want to apologise to you, lass. Mrs Sturdy would be turning in her grave if she knew I'd let things get to this.'

Grace was shocked. 'No apology needed, Mr Sturdy, none of it was down to you.'

He packed his pipe and lit it, sucking so hard on the stem she expected it might break off any minute and disappear down his neck.

'You did a fine job saving Ruby, we all think that. I've had a talk with the young fella who helped get her out of the water and he'll have nothing more to say on the other matter.'

Silence settled on the room.

He shifted in the chair as though to leave but instead looked directly at her.

'Grace, I'm terribly sorry. I was so caught up with the ship running aground and all the while you were standing there in front of my desk and I failed to see you were floundering too. If ever anything's worrying you again, I want you to bring it to me and we can talk about it. Or if you can't come to me, being a man and all, I want you to go to Joyce or one of the women.'

He sucked again on the pipe and the spark in the bowl of tobacco sprang to life. As he blew out the smoke it drifted in cotton balls between them.

He let himself out, telling her to come back to work when she was good and ready, he'd cope until then.

Lillian was next to visit, staying only ten minutes before it was time to ring the afternoon bell but long enough for Grace to see they'd become friends.

Joyce arrived mid-afternoon to deliver a large pot of pea and ham soup and a half-loaf but wouldn't stay, after which Grace napped for an hour in the chair. She was heating up the soup around five when Tommy knocked and asked how she was. It had been a week of surprises so it seemed only natural to invite him over the threshold and get out a second bowl.

She declined his offer to help. While she sliced and buttered the bread, he began making small talk, and then, at her prompting, he told her a little about how he'd come to be at Low Head.

He wasn't a career man in the lighthouse service

but had landed the job at the station after serving an apprenticeship with a joinery shop that'd gone bust in the city. His parents farmed on the East Coast, mostly sheep, and he went home for a week each Christmas, joined by a brother, two sisters and their families for the big day.

Grace didn't have much energy for chatting and left the conversation to Tommy, who stalled for a bit and then decided to stick with family stories.

He was the youngest, raised secure in the fact that one of his parents or three older siblings would come to his aid when needed. His brother had the bunk above his and every night read him a story. When he fell into the farm dam, his older sister fished him out. One wet winter he caught pneumonia and his mother didn't leave his side, sleeping on a mattress on the floor.

Grace could see how such a trusting childhood might incline a person to a cheerful disposition.

When he invited her to take a turn, she meant to put him off but her mouth opened and out came the rescue home — prayers at night, charity clothes, the schooling, and three square meals a day. She left out the rest because he didn't need to know about what she lacked, at the home and afterwards at South Arm. It made for a much shorter description of growing up than the one he'd provided.

They finished their soup and she offered him a chocolate from the bag Ruby had given. He chose a peanut cluster, and while she was deciding on a coffee crème, he reached into his pocket and unwrapped a clean handkerchief. He held it towards her in his open palm.

In the centre was a small carved bear, sitting on its haunches, paws holding a tiny fish. Tommy had carved it from King Billy pine, and a whorl in the pinkish timber spun out from its chest and around the body.

The bear was unexpectedly light in her hand. 'Thought maybe it'd be something interesting to look at on your mantle, or …' The rest of the sentence dangled mid-air while he took one long breath. '… you could keep it for the baby.'

When he'd gone, she washed up the dishes and damped down the fire for an early night. She would return to her work in the morning. She placed the bear on the windowsill in the living room and left it in the dark.

In bed, she drew the blankets in tight. That day in the river, close to drowning, she hadn't given up but given in. They weren't the same, not in anyone's book, but what difference it made she couldn't tell.

The head and the heart might not wish for the same thing and it was impossible to fathom which should take the lead.

She thought of the toddler Tommy, safe in the bosom of family on his farm while she squalled in a dormitory lit by a single globe. She felt no envy for his good fortune, though she'd had none. A child was seed thrown down in earth tilled by others, made rich with warmth and the right fertiliser like Tommy's, or left sparse and stony, like the ground on which she'd germinated.

The baby's foot let fly, as if to underscore the point. Rolling over, she pressed her belly to the bed but could not push away the unhappy thought that, at eighteen years old, she was no longer the child with circumstances out of her control. Like it or not, she was now the one to cultivate the soil.

Her daily routine resumed. She took the Superintendent's word and didn't rush it, doing only what she could manage the first few days while the pain and weakness in her arms, legs and lungs subsided. His routine had reasserted itself too, and he was gone to the office in the mornings by the time she made it to his door.

The following week, Lillian beckoned her over to the school. The son of the second pilot required extra coaching for an upcoming exam. His parents were keen he might eventually obtain work that wasn't dependent on weather and tides and were hopeful he might be accepted by the state school in Launceston to study for the Intermediate Certificate.

'It'd be a great help if you could watch the children for half an hour at the end of Tuesdays and Thursdays while I take him over his work for the next few weeks. I've talked to Mr Sturdy and he's agreeable as long as you are. I'd set them exercises, of course, so you'd only need to provide supervision.'

Walking the row of desks the first afternoon, Grace fancied herself an assistant teacher. It had a nice ring to it, but only if she ignored the fact that she couldn't turn side-on in case she got stuck between two desks.

Ruby's rescue had brought with it a respect she hadn't been shown as a cleaner, cook and a wayward pregnant girl. It was evident in the interactions as she moved about the pilot station. In reality, the larger portion of change did not come from the others but from her. She was letting her barriers down, just a little, and others stepped forward to meet her where she stood. Not everyone, of course, but she was less aloof and most responded in kind.

The downside was that the women were more emboldened to inquire about her health and ask how the baby was doing, which served to reinforce what the daily movements were making plain, that this was a living, breathing entity within.

As she entered her eighth month, Joyce sat her down to have a talk.

'Might be an idea to take the day off and get the bus to Launceston to get a few things in. Nappies, singlets, a couple of blankets and the like. The baby'll need them no matter what.'

Grace shook her head. She wasn't discounting the value of the woman's advice but it was still difficult to get her head around what might happen after the birth. She'd imagined, endlessly, entering the midwifery home, but all she could see was the door opening to a wide, dark tunnel she would hurtle through like the day on the train. On good days, she saw herself plunging out the other side, relieved of the creature, stomach flat. The other days, she never left the tunnel at all.

'I'm not saying you should keep the baby, Grace, but best to be prepared. It'll make it easier for you when the time comes.' Joyce was doing laps around the topic, uncharacteristically stubborn, refusing to drop it.

'If you want the baby adopted out, Nurse Woolley knows what to do and I'll support your decision. If you choose to keep him or her, we're all here to help you raise the child, and Mr Sturdy will make allowances for any limitations on your time.'

Grace was motionless, rooted to the spot, and Joyce reached over and squeezed her hand, misunderstanding the muteness as a sign she was considering the choice she might make.

Grace was most definitely in thought, but not about the final decision. She'd pulled up short in the moment when Mrs Jacques had referred to 'him or her' and in quick succession, 'the child'.

The baby, the newborn, the bundle wrapped in Mary's arms, the rhythmic rise and fall of the tiny chest in her arms. This wasn't a demon attached to her placenta but a human being, innocent and feeble and deserving of more than a wall of hate. If she could not love this child, she should give it away to people who would. She never said a word to Mrs Jacques; she didn't need to. The sobbing in the woman's ropey arms was sufficient explanation for them both.

She took the day off the following Wednesday, leaving early in the car with the Superintendent on his way to the monthly Lighthouse Service meeting. He would finish late so she planned to catch the bus back at two o'clock.

In Launceston, she was careful not to get lost. She bought expensive nappies, two shawls and two sets of baby clothes, reasoning that if adopted, the baby would take the items with it and she had given it the best start. She suffered the congratulations from the saleswoman but saw her sneak a look at her left hand, bereft of any wedding ring.

On the return trip, she took a seat at the front of the bus and more than once, as the coach rattled along, her chin dropped to her chest. Waking from the wooziness of semi-dozing, with the baby rotating under her ribs, it struck her like a blow. Come what may, babe in arms or not, by the middle of next month she'd be a mother.

Behind her, maybe even on the seat, she dare not look, was her own formless mother, and further back, the woman who'd given birth to her, then behind that woman another mother and so it went, a string of mothers reaching back, an unbroken line through eternity.

And what was forward?

It was the place already made where Grace would go to join them. There was no avoiding it.

The Tamar spread in a sluggish side-wash at this point in the river and she forced herself to give it her full attention.

Tommy was waiting when the bus reached the turning circle, half a mile from the pilot station, and he helped her carry the parcels home. They often bumped into each other as they went about their days, though she'd never repeated the invitation to a meal.

When he offered his arm for her to lean on, she took it with gratitude, and as they strolled up the road towards the pilot station gate, she forgot herself for a moment and rested her head on his shoulder as they walked.

'I'm pleased you can come back here after the birth, Grace,' Tommy murmured.

She straightened her head but felt no need to remove her hand from his arm. There was a word to describe the feeling and she searched through a few before she found the one that suited. She rolled it around on her tongue. *Companionable.* 'Yes, I'm grateful to Mr Sturdy. He's been very kind to me.'

Tommy nodded. 'I'm not surprised, he thought the world of your dad.'

Her mind was playing tricks. She stopped and swung around to face him.

'Who?'

The question burst from her with such force that

Tommy stepped back, puzzled at first, followed by a slow dawning that Alf Sturdy had kept this to himself, he might have his reasons.

'Grace,' he pleaded, 'I thought you knew.'

Tommy had no more to tell, claiming that what little he knew was hearsay and the matter was too important for gossip. The man who was supposedly her friend had refused to say anything further, urging her to speak to the Superintendent.

In her cottage, she unpacked the baby supplies, tortured by the knowledge that her life at the pilot station might be a lie, that people she'd come to trust had misled her. Alf Sturdy had not seen fit to share such vital information. She cast her mind back to the two of them in the café when he'd offered her work. At the table, there'd been a third chair, empty, or so she'd thought, but all the while there'd been a secret sitting there between them.

The Superintendent would not return until midnight, so she couldn't ask her questions until the morning. After eighteen years without answers, it was not much of a wait, she consoled herself. As she climbed into bed, however, it mattered little that this was the closest she'd been to finding out about her father. The big hand on the clock shuddered around each circuit it made, and despite her best efforts, she couldn't talk herself out of the agitation crawling underneath her skin.

At the first decent hour, she knocked on Joyce's door. She'd managed to wait until the children had left for school, but the polite thing would have been to forestall the visit, at least until Mrs Jacques had washed up from breakfast, made the beds and had the house more presentable.

Joyce's eyebrows shot up when she saw it was Grace. 'My, you're out and about early. Come in.'

Mrs Jacques wasn't one for small talk, but even if she were, Grace was at a loss to find any but the critical words she'd waited all night to disgorge. She couldn't contain them a minute longer. 'Mr Sturdy knew my father, or so I'm told. Have you heard anything about that?'

Joyce pulled out a chair and sat, gesturing for Grace to take one as well. Grace, however, needed to feel the floor under her feet and remained standing. The older woman was quiet under the burden of the question, and for a moment, Grace thought she might refuse to answer.

'It was a long time ago, Grace. Your father was in the service and they worked together, Mr Jacques too.'

Grace decided she needed the chair after all and, shifting her round belly to one side, dropped to the seat.

So they all had lied, Tommy, the Superintendent and now, of all people, Joyce. The secret was like thread in a tangled ball of yarn — the harder Grace tugged to unravel it, the tighter the knot in the wool.

'I don't believe Mr Sturdy lied to you, Grace. Yes, he chose not to mention it; but overlooking something is not the same as a lie.'

He'd suggested Joyce not speak of it either and she'd almost given the game away the first day when they'd met.

'You'd told him what you knew, which was very little. He could see you weren't in a good way and, what with your condition, he was afraid it'd be too upsetting to set you straight.'

No allowance, then, for the festering hurt at her centre where the truth should've been. She reminded herself she was far too young to be getting bitter or acting like a victim. And yet, everyone knew what was best for Grace Anderson except herself.

Joyce had little choice but to explain, Grace made sure of that.

It went back nearly two decades. The three men had worked alongside each other in the wild fury of West Coast weather, manning the Hells Gates lights in the teeth of the roaring forties at the mouth of Macquarie Harbour.

'Wives, too. We were all living on Entrance Island, just inside the harbour: Mrs Sturdy, myself and, of course, your mother.'

Grace didn't move, didn't even blink. After all the years of wondering, it was that simple. You sit at a table on a cloudy morning and just like that, someone raises the dead.

11

Joyce refused to say another word about it, loyal as she and her husband were to the Superintendent.

'I'm fond of you, Grace, and I'm not wanting to keep anything from you, but you need to talk to him first, love. He's the one to answer all your questions.'

Grace walked out without closing the door, would have stormed out but her lumbering gait held her back. She crossed the grass towards her cottage but changed her mind and headed up the path. The baby thumped low in her abdomen and at the same time, dragged a head or a limb across the height of the bulge, as if it was looking for the exit. *Both of us need to escape.*

Her energy jangled in all directions at once, fighting itself. Inside the Superintendent's cottage, she was close to hysteria. She needed to bring order through work. She got out the white vinegar, found an old newspaper and began cleaning the windows, though they'd only been done the week before. Her arms strained when she rubbed the glass up high and her breath was short, but she ignored both and kept on with the job.

She boiled water and then filled the mop bucket and cleaned the floor, getting onto her hands and knees to work the scrubbing brush and soap into the boards near the stove where food had spilled. She paused only when she had a dizzy spell, causing her to sit on her haunches momentarily. As she did, her elbow banged the bucket and sudsy water slopped out onto her lap. She ignored it, leaving the dirty stain to spread down her front.

Usually she'd put the kettle on around ten o'clock and stop for a cuppa and a biscuit or a piece of cake, whatever she'd made for the Superintendent to take to the office. She didn't bother looking at the clock and kept working. Moving was what mattered. Stopping only stranded you on the edge of the void, a shifting, shapeless mess of agony and nothingness.

She was so determined to stay busy that it was two o'clock before she looked out the door and saw the Superintendent's car at the office. It was then she let in her exhaustion after the morning's frenzy and sat for a while to rest. She was relieved to find that in all of the work, her thoughts had come to heel.

Usually, she'd do the downhill trip from the lighthouse to the main part of the pilot station in a few minutes, but today was slow. She felt like a man on death row going to his execution. The Superintendent understood a great deal more than her and perhaps — it hadn't crossed her mind in all the turmoil from before — the facts about her parents might prove too much to bear.

A foot or hand caught her under the ribs and she paused on the path and placed her hands on the small of her back to lift up her frame so she could take a deeper breath. She looked across the hipped roofs of the houses to the river. With the sun obscured by heavy cloud, the water had a muddy hue but advanced at full speed, regardless, towards the roar of the surf.

When she knocked and opened the office door, the Superintendent was on the phone and waved her in. She entered tentatively. Wherever the tide of the truth might lead, there'd be no return.

THE BABY HAD been more active than usual for a couple of days. Grace was past pretending she was carrying it like a heavy item in her shopping bag. She had at least allowed for the fact that it was a young creature, like the kitten given to Ruby in the hope it might take her mind off the nightmares. It wasn't as if the image of Clem's stony face had faded, more that the life inside her was becoming its own separate thing.

It was a surprise, when she struggled up off the bed, to discover that her centre of gravity had dropped. Somewhere during the night, the baby had worked its way south and she now had a gap between her ribcage and belly. Joyce had warned her this would happen and not to be worried, that it would be a sign the baby was getting ready for birth. Grace let out a groan. The baby might be ready but she wasn't.

She had stayed in her own cottage the day before, on the Superintendent's orders, resting and feeding herself the gooey comfort of porridge, golden syrup pudding, whatever took her fancy, digesting what she could of what she'd learnt. Joyce had sat with her for a while, doing what she did best, being there quietly without inquiry.

Tommy had tried to visit but she turned him away at the door, not because she didn't want to see him but because she did. She knew there was a good chance she might rest her head on his shoulder again, then everything would tumble out. And there was a need, for now, to keep it close until her father became more real. As for her mother, she must set her aside a little longer. It was much harder to put flesh on a spectre.

Right at the beginning, the Superintendent had said it was a big load of a story to carry and best to take it step by step.

'I'll tell you all I know, lass, I owe you that much. But there's plenty of time to find your way in it. No hurry, Grace, it's not going anywhere.'

Her father had a name — Jack, a solid sound, a name that was definite from start to finish. He had a job, assistant lighthouse keeper. He had a reputation, as a hard worker with his head screwed on the right way. He had a brave heart. But that was far too much to think about right now.

She dressed in the shift that once had been loose but now stretched tight around her middle. She wasn't hungry, though fried herself an egg and ate toast just the same because the baby would need the nourishment.

It was an effort to stand at the basin and wash the dishes but she did it anyway, leaning two or three times to stop herself swaying. Her back ached, pinched nerves radiating pain down her legs.

The baby hadn't moved since Grace had woken. For months it had made its presence known, day and night. Pockets of pressure up and down, pushing, pummeling, slinging an arm here or a leg there, flopping in full body rolls. The absence of action was strange, left her feeling oddly empty.

For the second time in a week, she knocked at Joyce's door far too early.

Within a few hours she was at the midwifery hospital, waiting for the duty nurse to show her to a bed. There had been no tunnel as she entered, only a long corridor with rooms either side and stairs at the end.

Nurse Pope had required her to strip off her clothes and wear a flimsy cotton gown with ties she couldn't reach to secure. The impractical garment flapped open as she climbed onto the bed and she wished that no-nonsense Joyce was still there, instead of in the car as the Superintendent drove them home.

'Still no movement, Mrs Anderson?'

Grace was thrown by the woman assuming she was married and was slow to answer.

'Mrs Anderson, I need you to help me here.'

As Grace answered the midwife's questions, which included intrusive queries about bowel movements and frequency, the nurse took out a wooden instrument with a pedestal base and a body shaped like a vase.

'Lift your gown, please.'

It was a pinard horn, she said, and would help her to detect if the baby had a heartbeat. Instinctively, Grace tensed and it hurt when the nurse placed the cold instrument near her navel and pressed her ear hard against it.

A familiar sensation was coming in like a rolling fog, pulling her away from the unwanted touch, from the breaching of her boundary. The desire to disappear was strong but she fought against it, determined to stay present. The child was probably dead and she was the only one who could receive the news.

The nurse removed the horn and began working her hands across sections of Grace's exposed belly, kneading it, rocking it lightly. Then she began at the pubic bone and repeated the same motion all the way to the ribs. 'Your babe's in position, no doubt about that. The head is well engaged.'

The examination room was cool and Grace was aware she'd begun to shiver.

The nurse took up the horn again and placed it to the right but lower than before. She looked at Grace and shook her head. She transferred to the opposite side, straining to listen. Against her will, Grace found herself urging the baby to move.

The nurse palpated the belly once again, more firmly this time. Grace thought she felt a slight flutter, but then there was nothing. Twice more the midwife listened with the horn, while Grace lay suspended in the silence that had descended in the room.

Months of hating the thing growing inside, of wishing it away, and now she lay on her back, knees pulled up, and wanted nothing more than to know it was alive.

Five more minutes went by, when the midwife, head on the earpiece, spoke. 'Ah, there you are, hiding you little rascal.'

In her opinion, part of the problem was that Grace had an anterior placenta, which turned out to mean that instead of attaching to the back of the uterus it had attached at the front, making it more difficult to detect movement and heartbeat.

'Even so, the heartbeat's not as strong as we'd like,' she announced.

An hour later Doctor Grey arrived. He agreed with the assessment and determined it was best to bring on labour immediately.

A waterproof sheet was placed under Grace and he ruptured the membranes. In her disoriented state, Grace thought the stream flooding out between her legs might be river water that'd been stuck inside.

'Amniotic fluid,' the nurse confirmed.

The doctor departed, reminding the midwife he would come when she phoned. After the rush of fluid subsided, Nurse Pope led Grace to a room with three beds, one of which was occupied by a woman dozing. After she'd pulled a screen along the side of the bed, the nurse disappeared briefly, returning with a razor, soap and a bowl of warm water.

She had to issue the command three times before Grace drew up her knees and then let them fall open so she could be shaved. Before the nurse had even touched the top of her thighs, tremors were shooting through them. Grace steeled herself and forced her attention onto the midwife's stiff white cap so she wouldn't give in to the impulse to kick the woman and her bowl away. Even so, a gasp escaped through her clenched teeth.

'We'll do an enema once the labour starts. For now, you can put on your nightwear and get some rest.'

The minute the midwife left, Grace rolled onto her side and faced the wall, fist stuffed against her mouth and shoulders convulsing. Her body was not her own and she couldn't tell if she was sobbing for the present invasions or all the other times, flesh and spirit bleeding, out and on. She cried for the baby she'd been and the one about to have its turn, wept until she was both and neither.

She'd stood in the Superintendent's office for half an hour or so that day, his words buzzing around her like a swarm of summer midges. Now and then, they'd hung together in a fleeting shape or image, forming and reforming while she struggled to keep up. She saw waves rearing forty feet or more, slamming in against the narrow gap to the harbour. An island and lighthouse clinging to the spot where spent waves weakened into choppy water.

She saw the square chest of a man who was her father, but he had no face. Behind him, a woman less distinct blurred in salt spray and sea mist. The Superintendent's words were still clear. 'She gave her life for you.'

The crying had drained her. She lay like she was the

one on the mortuary slab and wished for the woman to appear, for a glimpse of the mother, a brief memory of skin on skin. Try as she might, the only solid thing she felt was the stiffness of her limbs. She yearned for the unknown past but had no more power to draw it to her than she had to stop the dreaded future.

Long after the evening meal was over and the light in the room had been switched off, she reached for her belly and felt the heat of the baby. Had she been at home, in her own bed, she might have crooned to it — far too late now, to be sure, finding a soothing voice in the end to reassure the child. Instead, she wordlessly mouthed the lullaby she'd sung in the dormitory when the younger ones couldn't sleep, patting her stomach in time with the rhythm of the lines.

Rock-a-bye baby. On the tree tops. When the wind blows, the cradle will rock. When the bough breaks, the cradle will fall …

Crashing down. All crashing down.

About an hour before sunrise the labour began, coming on fast. Once the contractions had closed in, Grace was transferred to the delivery ward, where a tray of shiny tools was laid out on a stainless steel trolley off to one side. The largest was a pair of tongs, four or five times the size of those she'd seen used for sugar cubes.

Had Grace been at the midwifery home two years earlier, she wouldn't have had any pain relief, Nurse Pope told her when she came on shift at eight o'clock. The night nurse had been older, more pious, and quick to share her view that God needed to hear the screams of women in childbirth so he could be sure Eve was paying for her sins.

The private midwifery hospital was a modern one,

however, and as the birth progressed, Grace was offered a handkerchief sprinkled with twenty or so drops of chloroform.

'What will happen if I use it?'

'You'll go to sleep and when you wake up, it'll all be over.'

Grace gripped the strap near her head while her history converged. In the tumult of stabbing muscles and uterus, she went to meet it, stripped of her defences by the pain. Girl forced into womanhood, loss grieving into change. Somewhere in the mess there was a vacancy, she knew it now, and filling it fast was an unfamiliar force that might be strength, but she didn't care if it had a name.

Here was a choice she was ready to make. Grace was writhing and scared, and she was decided. She would not reach for oblivion and abandon the baby. Still clasping the strap with one hand, with the other she pushed the handkerchief away.

'You'll be wanting it soon,' Nurse Pope warned as she checked the baby's heartbeat yet again.

A new midwife had begun her shift by four o'clock, when Doctor Grey was called for the delivery. The spasms left no gap in which Grace could rest but ran one into the other, a seamless agony now attacking her lower back, but still she'd refused the chloroform. Feet in stirrups, hair and gown soaked with sweat, she feared her body would rip apart.

She saw the nurse greet the doctor and while he scrubbed his hands, they murmured between them. Though she couldn't catch the conversation, the concern was unmistakeable.

'We need to get this baby out as soon as we can, Grace,'

was all she remembered the doctor say, as he took up a position at the foot of the bed.

An hour later, the head arrived, the body and legs following in a hot rush of blood. 'A little boy.' There were no cries as the midwife wrapped the baby in a towel, hurrying to a table where she sucked at a narrow tube and then began vigorous rubbing.

Grace attempted to sit up but the doctor stopped her. 'Lie still, Grace. We have to wait for the placenta.' He went over to the nurse and they stood with their backs towards her.

She had no idea what they were doing, but minutes later the baby made a feeble sound and the nurse left with him in her arms, without Grace even getting a glance.

Doctor Grey placed a hand on her shoulder. 'He's gone to the nursery. We need to get him warm. I'm not going to get your hopes up, Grace. We'll do everything we can but it's touch and go.'

The placenta had delivered and Grace was helped into a wheelchair and taken to her bed, where she was sponged down, helped into her nightie and given a bowl of broth. 'Bed rest for three days,' the midwife told her.

Grace wanted to resist, perhaps go to the child, but she was wrung out and hadn't the energy for argument. She fell into a deep well of sleep, staying submerged until breakfast was served.

Nurse Pope came in soon after with the news that the boy had barely survived the night and was still not strong.

She rubbed Grace's arm once or twice. 'It's amazing what a drop of brandy will do to get a baby breathing but after that, it's down to their lungs and heart.'

The doctor would need to give his approval if Grace

were to see the baby. He would be in mid-morning to check on her and the child.

At half past ten, Doctor Grey examined Grace and declared her in good shape, in the circumstances. He had already been to see the boy.

'He's a fighter and he's accepted a little milk from a bottle.' They would take her to him if she wished to breastfeed, starting at midday.

Doctor Grey, perhaps remembering his patient from the earlier incident and seeking to be kind, said more than he normally would. 'Chloroform is a marvelous invention, with great efficacy in relieving the stress of childbirth. In unusual cases such as these, however, it is sometimes wise that the mother stays conscious enough to push. You did well, Grace. He may not have lived had it been a forceps birth.'

Grace was dozing later in the morning when the nurse in charge pulled up a chair, paperwork in hand. 'We need to know what you've decided to do with your infant, my dear. If you're putting him up for adoption, best not to see him at all.'

Without waiting for a response and barely pausing to take in oxygen, she continued with the outline of arrangements: forms to be signed, the binding of Grace's breasts, the departure from hospital a day or two earlier than the mothers who needed to learn how to bathe and care for their baby.

'No need for you to stay. Without an infant to be cared for, you can continue with bed rest at home.' She thrust the clipboard and forms at Grace. 'I'll be back when you're done.' The rubber soles of her shoes squeaked on the polished floor as she retreated.

From the other side of the screen, Grace heard a

woman's voice, though she spoke in low tones.

'It's a big decision, love. Don't let her bully you into it.'

The effort of giving birth and the resulting exhaustion left Grace feeling like she'd been wound through the rollers on her mangle. The cotton sheets rubbed her skin as though they'd been threaded with metal shards. Every thought, every memory had been erased but for the flash of her baby's body as the doctor handed him to the nurse.

The clipboard was on her bedside table. The bell had rung for visiting time and she heard a man chatting with the patient in the next bed, about the new baby and how their toddler would react.

She closed her eyes briefly and when she opened them, Joyce was coming through the door carrying a posy of dahlias from her garden. The doctor had phoned with the news, and her husband, with some persuading, had brought her in. She settled in the chair beside Grace and glanced at the forms. 'You've decided? Not going to see him then, I expect.'

Grace had come to understand that with her friend, the economical use of language was a mere distraction. It was far better to listen for the tone. What she heard was regret.

'It's an awful lot to consider, Joyce, one way and another.'

Her friend nodded, patted her hand and remained quiet.

'He's still not strong but improved on last night. It's been hard to know what's best; however, I realised this morning that there's no certainty, at least not until I'm old and grey and looking back on all this.'

She would go one small step at a time.

'The nurse has said it's best not to go to him, but I can't know if I want to keep him till I'm there with him and see how it feels.' She looked at Joyce. 'Will you come with me now for a look?'

Grace rang the bell and when the nurse arrived with the wheelchair, Joyce helped her into it and they set off down the corridor to the nursery.

Nurse Pope was there, changing a nappy on a fretful four-day-old. 'Don't stay long. We don't encourage visitors in here with the babies.'

Grace's newborn was tightly swaddled in his iron bassinet.

'Oh Grace, your son is so like you.' It was a whisper, but still, Joyce hadn't meant it to be said out loud.

'Do you think? He seems like his own person, to me.'

It was a new experience, to speak and be surprised at what came out of her own mouth. It was completely true, she thought. The boy was not her. Finally, she dared to admit it. He was most certainly not Clem.

By the time Joyce had wheeled her back to bed, there was no decision to be made. It was already done, determined at the crib. She reached out and tugged on her friend's sleeve, leaning in. 'I'm going to bring him home.'

Joyce managed four words in the remaining time to the end of visiting hours. 'I am so pleased.'

Grace wanted to call him Jack, but it didn't seem fair to name him after another, dead or living. It was difficult to choose. She wanted him to have a name he could lean on, not like her own, mocking at every turn with its promise of God-given mercy.

She settled on a simple, solid name he could rely on: John. She'd call him Johnny until he had a chance to grow into it. It was as if the gift of a name was all the boy needed, because it seemed to Grace, from that point on, the infant began to thrive. He took easily to the breast and she found long hours of satisfaction in watching his bliss as he sucked in the milk while perfect butterfly hands brushed across her skin.

The nurse in charge made her position known, loudly informing Grace she was not yet twenty-one and in the eyes of the law, incapable of adult decisions. The nurse's robust efforts were thwarted more than a little by the doctor's kindness and in the end had no effect.

After ten days, Doctor Grey declared mother and baby fit to travel and the Superintendent arrived and drove them to Low Head. Grace sat in the front, the babe asleep on her lap. With so much needing to be said between them, she and the Superintendent took the safest course and said nothing.

At the pilot station, he drove past her cottage and up to his front gate. He went inside and returned a few minutes later with the cradle. Such tenderness, Grace hadn't seen it in him before, as he loaded it into the car and then took mother and baby home.

Only when he'd helped her inside and set the cradle on the floor did he speak to the boy, tucking a pound note into his shawl. 'May it be the beginning of much good fortune in your life, young John.'

He lit the fire in the stove and built it up. Joyce had left a pot of stew on the doorstep and he got it on to warm before saying goodbye.

'You won't stay to share a meal?'

'No thanks, lass. I'll be on my way. You two need time to settle in. Joyce'll be over in the morning, if there's anything you need.'

Grace changed Johnny's nappy and then sat in the fireside chair and fed him. The cottage was different somehow. It wasn't because of the cradle or the bag of nappies spilling out on the table or even the baby's loud gulping, she was sure of it.

Everything around her had a sharper quality. She wondered if this was how it was when a person with poor sight had spent years in a blurry world and then one day was given spectacles.

While the baby slept, she left the nappy soaking in the laundry before ladling out stew. It pleased her to see Johnny cosy in the cradle, its wooden sides protecting him from any draft, and she nudged it with her foot to see it rock. Long ago, another foot had set it rocking and she thought of Mrs Sturdy and the mothering cut short.

She was sad, then. Not for her young self and all she'd lost, though she felt it keenly still. The sorrow stealing through her heart was new. She was standing on the other side of pain, feeling distress for her mother, cut off forever from the baby she'd grown.

Her mother was in her, in the meat of who she was, as Grace was in Johnny and his cells. She watched the flames flare as they caught a fresh piece of wood, a burst of heat warming her face. Her mother waited, locked in time. She must find a way to her, for surely her spirit hadn't died.

She stacked the baby's clothes and nappies on the shelf in her bedroom, washed her face and changed for bed. She waited for Johnny to wake for his feed. Life was not a river, forced in one direction to the sea. It could flow two ways, child to parent, parent to child. She had spent close to nineteen years craving, pining for the bottomless need of mother and father, and now they asked for something in return.

She was fearful, for sure, but what did an old wound matter when the scar allowed the limb to move. She would speak again to Mr Sturdy and see the story through.

12

Ruby's mother arrived mid-morning with the gift of her old pram. It was a snug fit but could be stored in the laundry between outings, and maybe Tommy could fix the hood. After so many days in bed, Grace needed to build up her muscles again and she fed Johnny and then pushed him up the path to the Superintendent's cottage.

The Superintendent had made an effort to tidy but the standard wasn't high, so while the baby dozed, Grace took her time doing the dishes, sorting out the bedroom and gathering up dirty clothes, tea towels, and the tablecloth she'd put out a fortnight ago. She would tackle the copper tomorrow and perhaps cook him a meal, but that was enough for today.

Alf Sturdy was a good man; she had no cause to doubt it anymore as she set about restoring order in his cottage. He hadn't taken her in to set things right, walking a high road to moral ground. It had been more practical than that. The day he'd opened up, it was plain for her to see that he laboured under his own load of pain and bringing her to Low Head had been his way to live with it.

The night of the incident had begun like any other on Entrance Island, he'd said. There'd been some issues with the mantle but it was burning well, watched by Jack Anderson on the lighthouse bridge, an hour into his shift. Mr Sturdy and his wife were in their house, preparing for bed.

The SS *Kawatiri* was a former collier, fitted out as a passenger steamer and doing the run between Hobart and the West Coast. She'd left the capital in early afternoon and was ploughing through heavy weather near Macquarie Heads with forty passengers, eleven crew, several bags of mail for the port at Strahan and local mining towns, and a cargo of timber and coal.

The Captain had checked the nearby signal at Cape Sorell, which showed a red light, and noted that it indicated an ebb tide and sixteen feet of water on the bar. He'd gone in on exactly the same signal the week before.

'It's all there, Grace. Everything you need to know. In the trunk.' The Superintendent had tried to send her up to the cottage right then but she'd refused to go.

'I can't. I need to hear it from you.'

A westerly gale was howling through the dark as Captain Crawford headed for the narrows, where a long rock wall had been built to funnel the water's force, so it scoured a reliable channel.

'The thing is, Jack had no idea your mother was on the ship that night.'

The sudden intrusion of Grace's mother, in the midst of the Superintendent's description of the scene, had hit Grace like a bolt of lightning.

Amy Anderson, who'd turned thirty a month earlier, had been in Hobart attending to matters outside the bounds of what could be addressed in a remote location. As fate would have it, she'd argued with the cousin where she'd been staying and had chosen to return early.

Grace remembered the launch engines roaring into life at the nearby jetty as the Superintendent reached this part of his telling.

'She was coming home with you and your older brother.'

Until eleven o'clock on that August night in 1907, Grace had been part of a family.

Johnny was now stirring, screwing up his face as he worked his way to the effort of crying. Grace edged the pram down the two steps and closed the cottage door, wheeling the baby away from the room, the blackwood table and the trunk below it.

She paused for a moment, despite the baby's bursts of protest, and scanned the river before glancing back over her shoulder at the lighthouse tower. Whiter than the scudding clouds, it soared towards the sky and in a trick of perspective, leaned towards her. For a moment, she thought it might come to life and whisper in her ear.

The tower and all the others like it on the godforsaken islands and the treacherous coast around Tasmania were her bloodline. They'd been there with her in the womb, the egg dividing to the pattern laid down by her parents and the towers' story. She was a daughter of the light.

Like her mother, she'd been born in the shadow of a lighthouse, her grandfather a captain on the Kent group of islands, stark granite outcrops in the strait.

'Your mother knew the wild sea and its ways. She wouldn't have been afraid as they crossed the bar. She'd have been watching the two of you sleep and waiting to reach the wharf at Strahan.'

The Superintendent had faltered then in his recounting and although Grace had wanted him to blurt the rest out, she let him stand at the window and fill his pipe, and then keep circling the edge of the incident.

'The bar was the only seaward access. Convicts imprisoned years before on a speck of island at the top of the harbour were forced to row it. They called it Hells Gates. The weather and ocean often raged so the name stuck.'

Over time, the lights on Entrance and nearby Bonnet Island, the signal station and the breakwater had been built to keep ships safe. It'd been nine years since the last shipwreck.

'The crossing was a risky business but we thought we had it beat after '98. A terrible year, when heavy seas took two. The *Grafton*, she lost a propeller, but went down without loss of life. She carried a loco for the Mt Lyell mine railway, and some of its parts are still buried in the sand.'

Maybe it was the look on her face but he seemed to realise he'd strayed too far from events of the night. He'd looped back to the story.

Most *Kawatiri* passengers had been in their bunks when a rogue wave reared up and slammed the ship. It was flung against the breakwater, where it shuddered on the rocks from bow to stern, decks flooding. The next wave dragged her off and tossed her like a toy onto the dangerous North Spit, where she stuck fast, water pouring below.

'The Captain gave the order for the crew to get all the women and children onto the bridge deck while the boatswain launched the lifeboat, shouting directions over the shrieking of the engine room bell. It was cold; most were scantily clad, some with babes in arms like you. Twenty-two souls in the lifeboat that night when the first mate aimed it at the Entrance light. We could hear the screams over the roar of the wind.'

The Superintendent had stuttered to a halt and she'd had to beg him to go on.

It had been difficult to listen to it all, but now, weeks

later with Johnny in her arms, she was no longer standing alongside the others and watching from the island. She was the babe and mother all in one, out on the angry sea.

Day by day, Grace was finding her way to a new routine, caring for the baby, cooking and cleaning up the hill. At night, she inched her way into the hell at Entrance Island, the deafening wind, the smell of panic in the lifeboat.

Halfway to the island, huge breakers had swamped the escaping passengers. The first mate saw the stewardess washed overboard, crying out grievously as she was swept away. He didn't know that Amy Anderson and five-year-old William had gone too. Whether it was desperation or intuition, she had thrust the baby at one of the seamen seconds before.

The lifeboat hit smooth water for a moment. Free of the snarl of waves, it was snagged by the tide. The force propelled it onto the breakwater, smashing it against the rocks. Two of the sailors jumped out and ran off, abandoning the passengers to their fate. Immediately, a surge grabbed the boat and flipped it up, flinging people out.

In the mad scramble, some made it onto the wall. One of the lightkeepers saw a woman sinking and hauled her out by the hair. The signalman waded repeatedly into the water and dragged to land several women and children who were struggling. In the dark, men from the island ran along the top of the breakwater, helping where they could. Mr Sturdy had found a toddler limp on the rocks and thought him dead, sprinting with him to the closest house where, miraculously, he revived.

Grace's mother and brother were last seen about fifty feet from the end of the breakwater, the sea slowing briefly with them in its grasp before snatching them away. Her father, his entire family at stake, was stuck on duty in the tower.

It was probably a good thing, Grace thought, that the Superintendent's throat had closed after that. She needed time to find her way. She'd taken it all in, no problem with that, but it had lodged leaden in her gut, a lump as hard as a chunk of coal and just as black.

Mrs Sturdy evidently had done her best to care for Grace that night and in the days that followed, while Jack Anderson became a hollow man.

'We did what we could for him, Grace, but it pained him to watch over the waterway where they drowned. After a while, he wasn't fit to work.'

He'd been transferred to Low Head and Grace taken to the rescue home, a temporary measure until her father recovered. 'He always intended to come back for you.'

She'd asked the Superintendent then if he was still alive.

'There's things that are worse than dying, lass,' was all that he would say.

It played on her mind, as the weeks rolled by.

Tommy visited after work to fix the pram.

'What would it take, to break a man?' Grace asked him.

He had no answer, shaking his head and taking a screwdriver to the frame of the hood.

A pair of shoes once a year was a pitiful replacement for a father. She could never imagine, now she'd come to care, what could cause her to hand Johnny over. Such a fierce love now it had flowered, there was no room to spare for doubt or backing off.

She needed to talk. With the repair done, she surprised Tommy by inviting him in for a slice of beef pie and the chance to continue the conversation.

'You can't know what's in a man's heart,' he said, shoveling in the food. 'That's the only place that can give any answers.'

Later, he held the baby, dancing a gentle jig to quiet the fretful child while she prepared the bedding in the cradle. Each busy with their own task, he took the chance to be bold.

'It wasn't you he left, Grace. He was running from himself.'

While she settled Johnny, Tommy scooped tea leaves into the pot and boiled water. They sat at the table, drinking the strong brew while the baby snuffled and twitched his way to sleep.

They watched the peaceful rise and fall of the baby's chest and confined their chat to the happenings of the day. Tommy had said all that she could bear.

As easily as a weather change coming in from the Strait, they shifted in their friendship. A forecaster would have picked it as a high-pressure system, bringing predictable conditions. Tommy began eating at the cottage a couple of times a week, sometimes more, often arriving with a gift he'd fashioned for Johnny: a teething peg, a wooden truck, a tiny spinning top.

He never stayed long, only enough to wash up their dishes while she fed the boy or put him to bed. So one night when he lingered, she knew he had something to say.

'It's plain, I reckon Grace, that I want this to be more. But it can never be while ...'

His voice petered out, leaving in its wake a sick feeling in her belly. Of course it was impossible, taking on damaged goods and a bastard son. She was doing what she always did so well, pretending not to see.

She saved him from the need to finish the sentence; spared herself the pain.

'I know, Tommy, and I don't think any the worse of you for saying it. You've been a good friend, even when I was doing my darndest to stop you. Your family will want the best for you and you should, too. Johnny and I will be just fine on our own.' She turned away, stirring the fire to hide her dismay. When she glanced back around he had shock on his face.

'You've got it all wrong.' He held out one hand, palm up as though to push her away. 'It's clear you don't know me at all.'

With that, he was gone, yanking the door behind him but at the last minute shoving his shoulder against it to stop it banging. It bounced off his body and Grace stepped in to close it while the baby slept on.

The pilot station was a small settlement; however, they managed to avoid each other for the rest of the week.

The following Friday, Joyce was approaching Grace as she carried the baby out her door. It was obvious that she'd noticed Tommy, on his way to the supply ship at the jetty, catch sight of mother and babe and dive back towards the workshops.

'You two fallen out?' she asked, lifting Johnny for a cuddle.

When Grace ignored the question, her friend let it lie, storing it to one side along with what had transpired in the Superintendent's office weeks before.

Grace knew Joyce wouldn't pry, though there'd been times as she raked over the events of that August night at Macquarie Heads, she'd wished Mrs Jacques had tried.

Her table was a lonely place without Tommy on the other side, so she took to eating her meal in the fireside chair, the plate balanced on her lap, never looking further ahead than the next load of dirty nappies or the shopping list to write.

Johnny mostly woke to be fed around three in the morning and sometimes, in the cold early hour as she tended to him, she'd search his face for signs of Clem. Finding none, her mind would journey into other dark corners it avoided during the day.

She thought often of her mother and brother in the boat and the split second that separated her from them. An increment of time, infinitesimal, yet the distance it measured went on forever. The sea had meant to claim her too, but Amy Anderson had ruined its plans.

The times when Grace had given herself over to the water, had she been seeking her mother, was that the welcoming presence she'd found? It played on her mind that there was still so much she didn't understand and the worst part was that the more facts she gathered in the outer world, the less she knew herself on the inside.

A few days later, as she left the Superintendent's cottage, a sharp squall cut in across the river and she was glad the pram hood worked so she could pull it up to shelter Johnny. Winter was making a pre-emptive strike, icy winds chasing off sunny early mornings and the thermometer dropping rapidly in the afternoons.

She kept her head down to stop the rain from stinging her eyes as she pushed the baby home. She'd just wedged the pram into the laundry and was coming out with Johnny in her arms when Tommy appeared in front of her.

'I'm still angry, Grace, but I can't go avoiding you

forever.' He followed her inside, taking the baby while she removed her coat and put fresh kindling in the stove, setting a match to it.

She was at a loss to know what to do or say.

He handed the baby back but when she offered him a chair he said he wouldn't stay. 'I don't know much about the world and its ways, Grace, but this …' He opened his hands wide and turned his head in both directions to take in the room. 'This is not enough.'

It'd been a long while since she'd wanted to hit him, but she could easily do it now, slap him for his impudence.

'It might not look like much to you, with a farm, a cosy family, and money at your back. But it's taken all I have to get to this and unlike you, I've learnt to be grateful for what's given.' She'd shouted the final words, disturbing Johnny, and he began to grizzle. She placed him in the cradle and rocked it with a foot.

Tommy pushed a chair across so she could sit as she settled the baby.

'You can't keep doing this, hiding away from what you fear will hurt. It's a wall, Grace, and it keeps me out. This isn't about me and the kin I come from. It's about you and whether you can risk owning the family you've got.'

It was quite a speech from Tommy, but she could find nothing to say in her own defence; the heat had gone out of her.

He was quiet for a few minutes, and then took his leave.

She was awake far more than Johnny that night, relieved when he stirred and she could hold him, warm and hungry for her. He'd steadily increased his weight and after five weeks was on a growth spurt, eager for the breast every couple of hours during the day and waking to feed at least twice through the night.

He gave his whole body to the effort of drawing out milk, each sucking motion vigorous at his mouth and cheeks before fading down his trunk, sometimes ending with a soft shudder at his legs and feet. He was unashamed in his demand, full of wanting. A wave of pride, she thought it was that, came over her as she held one perfect hand. His life depended on his need and helpless as he was, he knew to go to meet it.

She fell into a deep sleep before dawn and woke later than usual, with Johnny still in the bed. By the time they left the house, storm clouds pressed low, bearing down on the two of them as they went up the path. She had barely bumped and dragged the pram inside when a thunderclap rattled the windows.

Within minutes, a downpour demolished the view and rain drummed on the roof so loudly not a sound could be heard from the workshops or the school. Grace worked on through the storm, cleaning a little and then preparing a meal. When the worst of it had passed, she had the absurd sense that it'd taken the pilot station with it and left her and Johnny behind. She stepped out briefly into light rain, reassured at the sight of houses still gathered around the square.

She continued to feel unsettled and finished work early but instead of going home, detoured to Joyce's place. Her friend was making quince jelly, pouring the pink, cooked fruit into a muslin-lined colander over a bowl. She tied the muslin at the top and took the bowl and colander out to the laundry, where the liquid would strain slowly overnight.

Returning to the kitchen, Joyce opened a tin of sardines

and slathered them on thick slices of bread, handing one to Grace, who was feeding Johnny.

Grace needed to talk. 'That night at Hells Gates, I don't need to tell you about it, Joyce, because you were there. Mr Sturdy explained what happened.'

Joyce nodded and continued to chew. Grace lifted the baby to her shoulder and he burped loudly, making the two women laugh.

She told Joyce about the trunk, how the Superintendent would only share so much of what he knew. Afterwards, she settled the baby in the pram and the two women spoke softly while they drank tea, about the groceries arriving late the day before and the improved mood of the boat crew now the new head pilot had settled in.

The tea finished, Grace pulled on her coat and reached for the handle of the pram, but Joyce stopped her.

'Leave him be, love. I'll keep an eye on him. Go over there — it's time to see what's in the trunk.'

It seemed heavier when she dragged it out. Curiosity from the first time was now replaced by dread. She took out the brooch and the christening gown, laying both on the dresser.

Next was a gold locket wrapped in tissue paper, the back engraved with the name of the Sturdys' first-born, and a yellow and white crocheted baby blanket. The stale smell was growing stronger as she took out a large framed photo of a young Alf Sturdy, smiling beside his dark-haired bride, and a fancy cardboard box with pressed flowers the young woman had preserved from her bouquet.

At first she thought the thick layer of newspaper at the bottom was packing, until a headline jumped out.

Cowardice of Sailors. Steamer Wrecked. Disaster With First Boatload.

Every sheet of newsprint held its own account, so many voices springing up from the shipwreck and its aftermath that Grace's head was spinning. She gathered the pile of clippings and began to lay them out in chronological order along the table.

With the task complete, she adjusted each one so the end of the columns was level with the edge of the table. Only then, when she could find no more call to bring order, did she begin reading.

She started with the article about the telegram arriving at the shipping company's Hobart office, where relatives wept openly for the lack of information about who was among the dead. And a telegram, hours later, to the Commissioner of Police saying six lives had been lost: the Stewardess, Mrs Anderson, her son and three other children.

The Superintendent had been so keen for her to see the newspaper articles and yet, as she continued to read, the accounts were consistent with what he'd said and it was odd that he'd sent her to the trunk. She persisted for another quarter of an hour and was about to pack them away when her eye fell on a story only four or five paragraphs long. *The Kawatiri Disaster: Pitiful Stories*

She wasn't sure if she got to the end because she was on her knees, sobbing so hard she thought she'd turn herself inside out.

Lighthouse keeper Anderson told the inquiry a pitiful story. He states that as he stood on the bridge of the lighthouse, he heard his wife screaming from the water. She was shouting 'Jack, save me' but he was powerless to afford any aid.

All he'd heard after that was the roar of the breakers thrashing on the bar.

Grace got to her feet. Despite a headache building behind her temples, she went back to her reading. She owed him that, and the mother and brother so cruelly torn away.

A diligent search for bodies went on for days.

It is probable that the bodies have been carried out to sea. As the coast is infested by sharks, there is little probability of the remains being recovered.

All the while, her father was sticking to the code of the lighthouse service, following the roster and doing his turn with the light.

Then seemingly from nowhere, the sea had returned them to him. A searcher found Amy Anderson's body wedged between two rocks near the tip of the cape. William's cold frame was still clasped to her chest.

Grace finally understood this would be the moment, no matter what the orders, when he'd quit the island.

After the funeral, he'd returned briefly but only to pack their scant furniture and belongings. He would take Grace across the bar one last time, to the rescue home in Hobart, then go north to Low Head.

She gathered up the clippings and repacked the trunk, leaving the newspapers on the bottom where she'd found them, and hurried out the door, red-eyed and desperate to hug Johnny.

Since the *Southern Star* had grounded, the Superintendent had been off-site uncommonly often. She'd hardly seen him for days on end, tangled as he was in the wash-up from the inquiry, interviews for the new pilot, briefings on changes to lighthouse service and marine board policies, and extra meetings.

It was almost a week before she spotted him in the office and she'd just entered when the coxswain knocked with something he said was urgent. The Superintendent asked her to return the next day, after he'd made the daily nine o'clock phone call to update Melbourne port on conditions at the river mouth.

Her sleep had become so ragged she often burned the lamp past midnight, waiting until Johnny woke in the wee hours to pick him up and crawl with him into bed. Under the covers, the baby made contented noises as he fed in the dark.

She lay with him on her chest and mourned her mother, clinging the same way to her child. Two different mothers with their sons, but all of them were flotsam on the fury of a running tide. Grace and Johnny swept along, not by a rushing channel of water but the surging charge of her stubborn streak.

Her mother had been brave, protecting one child and trying to save the other until the last. Grace, too, was out of her depth; however, all she had to do was set both feet firmly down and stake out dry land and a safe place for her son and herself.

It seemed so easy, as she dozed off to sleep with Johnny nestled at her breast. She could take a chance with Tommy, learn to trust.

Life was more complicated in the harsh light of day. She woke groggy, annoyed that she couldn't delay meeting with the Superintendent, that she would be expected at his desk in a couple of hours.

Despite having plenty of time, she arrived ten minutes

late, kicking the brake forward on the pram and leaving it and the baby outside the door. As she began the conversation with the Superintendent, Johnny began squawking, building up quickly to a squeal.

'Bring him in, love. He doesn't want to be left alone.'

She sat on a straight-backed chair, the baby on her lap, while the Superintendent swiveled sideways at his desk and listened as she shared what she'd found in the newspapers.

When she'd finished, she held his gaze. 'I need to know. You must tell me, please. Where is he now?'

The clock on the wall ticked loudly two or three times before he spoke.

'You 'n me both, Grace. It'd do us both good, I reckon, to deal with the truth.'

He began to address her and didn't stop for a quarter of an hour, not pausing for questions or even his pipe. When he finished, she sat in silence for a good while more, the baby asleep and dribbling on her shoulder.

'It's time for me to get to work,' was all she said.

As she wheeled the baby away, Jack Anderson was everywhere she looked. He'd worked mainly upriver with three other men, a couple of miles away at the leading lights. By the time Mr Sturdy had been promoted to Superintendent at the pilot station, nearly two years after the *Kawatiri* was wrecked, her father had been functioning a little better.

Occasionally he did a shift at the lighthouse, and it had been on one of those occasions that his life had taken a turn for the better. The Superintendent had hoped it would see him through to bringing Grace back from the rescue home.

13

The overnight temperature hovered around five degrees for weeks on end and in the Low Head houses, fires burned all day and much of the night. Tommy barrowed over a few loads of wood and stacked it against the back wall of Grace's cottage, greeting her politely as he worked. They had returned to their habit of brief chats when they bumped into each other and he always asked after the baby, but that was as far as it went.

Except for the walk to the Superintendent's cottage, it was too bitter for Grace to have the baby outside, especially when he'd developed a runny nose. Her life was passing by while she was chained to one kitchen or the other and, stuck inside, there was far too much time for thinking.

It turned out that her father had lived at Low Head twice, the first time at the leading lights and the second at the pilot station.

'He took leave to go and see you two or three times but he was always worse when he returned, rattled, unreliable on the job. We'd have to keep an eye on him,' the Superintendent had said. 'I don't think he could keep reliving it, so it was better to stay away. He did go to Hobart one more time, but that came later and, sorry lass, it wasn't to see you.'

Grace had already done the calculations. By the time she was about fourteen months old the visits had ended.

Walking the path to the lighthouse was as close as she

could get to her father now, knowing his boots had walked the same gravel, that he'd stood on the jetty and seen the same view.

Each passing ship was a reminder that she shared more with him than the loss of wife–mother and son–brother. She liked to think that she and Jack Anderson, each in their own way, were bound together by Low Head. It'd been different times and they played a different part, hers less direct, but they both contributed what they could to keeping the river mouth safe.

She wanted to soften to him, think kind thoughts, but no matter how often she searched for compassion, it was barred by steel.

While she'd languished in the rescue home, he'd been busy putting her behind him. She wanted to be fair and Lord knows, the Superintendent had tried to encourage it, but she was shaken by the sense that she'd been discarded.

'He was a man who knew how to love, and he loved the three of you so much, it wasn't good for him. You were the spitting image of Amy, he fell apart every time he saw you.'

So, her father had turned away long before the money stopped arriving. The hurt consumed her cottage, followed her everywhere she went at the pilot station and even to East Beach when she couldn't stand it anymore and had to flee. She bundled Johnny up in two blankets and pushed the pram fast, almost running across the headland to the bay; however, the minute she slowed the ache was there.

She crooned to the boy at night. 'You be kind and good when you grow up. And come what may, Johnny, you stand by the ones you love.'

Jack had gone on with his life, courting a woman more than ten years younger, the daughter of a pilot at Low

Head. He had married the twenty-year-old and in his renewed stability, the service had seen fit to post him far out into the strait.

He and his new wife started afresh on Goose Island, a narrow streak of granite so sparse its population was limited to little penguins, shearwaters and gulls.

As the Superintendent spoke, he still seemed to be circling something difficult. He talked of the island's isolation, about the mail that arrived once a fortnight, often at two in the morning. She'd tried to divert him back to her father but he'd ignored her, continuing on with the tale of everyone tumbling out of bed to light hurricane lamps while the assistants took to the oars and rowed out for the deliveries.

'The mail ship, she didn't stop, see. She only slowed down as she passed on the eastern side.'

It took some cajoling before Grace succeeded at last in guiding him back to the subject of her father. The Superintendent had risen from his chair and as he did, she'd seen a change cross his face. From then on, he'd pointed the story straight ahead and steered it directly into the wind.

Grace had found it hard to hear that her father and Eleanor had been happy and that soon his wife had been pregnant with twins. Grace figured that her younger self had been about four years old at the time and though she'd badly wanted to ask, she sensed that the Superintendent would not have known why Jack, with a new family, hadn't returned to claim her.

It mattered little, as events transpired. Eleanor was taken off the island early, due to the risk of having a premature birth. It proved prophetic. The pregnancy lasted only until twenty-seven weeks.

Jack followed her to Hobart, arriving the day the twins were born, but he didn't get to hold them; the girl and boy had died in the womb. The doctors worked for hours on Eleanor, who was bleeding heavily, but she went to meet her babies less than a day later.

For the second time, her father was left to arrange a funeral for his family.

The Superintendent had pulled some strings to get Jack off Goose Island and back to Low Head, where at least he'd have a community of folk around him.

'We did what we could, the wives too. But it was like a faultline opened up and day by day he fractured a little more.'

At first, the Superintendent had him working shifts at the lighthouse and he seemed to be doing okay. In the New Year, the Superintendent began getting reports that duties had been ignored or poorly executed and the steadiness of the light was at risk.

It was a step down, and no lightkeeper worth his salt would have willingly agreed to it, but he moved Jack to the maintenance crew. The Superintendent kept him on daytime work, looking after the acetylene gas plants, attending to fences around the quarters, unloading supply vessels, whitewashing walls, and building a new cowshed.

It grieved the Superintendent to see him decline. 'He resisted, you know, when I took him off the light. Said it wasn't right, that he knew his job and wanted to do more. Couldn't understand his mind was losing its thread.'

They'd limped along, the Superintendent making all the allowances that he could, the men grumbling about carrying an extra share of the load yet supporting Jack as one of their own. As the years passed, they got used to the way Jack drifted sometimes, unmoored in the present yet unable to live with the past. If he didn't always make sense, was occasionally erratic, who were they to judge?

In early summer 1917, the Superintendent heard violent shouts from the workshop and hurried over. Jack was barricaded in a corner, eyes blazing like the very devil, a stream of obscenities issuing from his mouth. He jabbed the air with one fist, and in its grip was a sharpened crowbar.

Grace, already struggling with her vision of a sorrowing father, had found it impossible to imagine the man unraveling.

It had taken four men to subdue him and remove the weapon, all the while Jack was panicked, screaming that they should keep away, he was evil and they'd all burn in hell with him.

They locked him in the Superintendent's cottage until Doctor Grey could examine him.

'We did it to keep him safe but it was a terrible thing, caging him like a wild beast.'

The doctor knocked him out with a sedative and then left to make some phone calls. Next morning, he returned to sedate Jack again so he could be taken away. The Superintendent declined the offer of an ambulance, insisting on driving him south himself.

At five o'clock that evening, Jack Anderson was declared a danger to society and admitted to the Mental Diseases Hospital at New Norfolk, about thirty minutes drive from Hobart.

'He was never fit to discharge. It weighs heavily on me, Grace, that I was the one who sealed his fate. A lifetime locked up.'

Alf Sturdy didn't cry, he didn't need to. The pent-up

emotion was expressed in the contortions of his face, the tremor in his hands.

He told Grace all he knew.

The male refractory ward was a century old. Dark, dismal, ill ventilated, it was no place for a man who'd lived by the sea. They took him to work in the mat-making and weaving room, but the chaos of his mind couldn't accommodate the order of a loom.

He'd escaped a few weeks later, running as far as the nearby town of New Norfolk before the police captured him and returned him to the asylum as the dinner bell rang. He was laced into a straitjacket and kept in the security ward for two days, after which they locked him in an isolation room for the rest of the week.

The Superintendent had visited six months later. The nursing staff frequently administered knockout drops, and the chloral hydrate subdued him but did little to stop his confusion. The drug was forced on him so often that sometimes he vomited or broke out in a rash.

The nurse in charge of the ward confided to the Superintendent that the medical super had recommended a lobotomy; however, Jack had been spared when the man resigned and his replacement banned the practice.

The Superintendent had visited once more, the following year, initially pleased to see his friend no longer incarcerated but on an open ward. Sitting with him, grappling for a few words to say, any pleasure had faded fast.

'He's a shell of a man, Grace. I couldn't go back. He's not your father anymore.'

THE PILOT LAUNCH was heading towards its mooring as Grace left her cottage with Johnny. As it tied up, two exhausted stormy petrels lifted up from their perch on the cabin and took flight towards George Town.

Through the schoolroom windows, she saw the heads of the children and at the front of the room, Lillian pointing to a large map on the wall. Grace had been distracted for months, settling into a rhythm with Johnny and slowly digesting the truth about her father. She hadn't spoken to Lillian for weeks and resolved to drop by on her way home that afternoon.

When she came back down the path, the door was closed and Lillian was nowhere to be seen. On Sunday morning, Rev. Babington held the fortnightly service in the pilot station's modest timber church. Lillian was there and as the congregation left, Grace sought her out and invited her home for tea and fruitcake.

By the time they'd reached the front gate, Lillian's face had a bluish hue and her breathing was laboured.

'Must have caught something. My energy seems to be lagging lately,' she said, before Grace had a chance to inquire about her health.

It was pleasant sitting near the fire, laughing while Lillian held Johnny upright and let him test his chubby legs on her lap, the baby waving his arms so excitedly that he banged a fist against his nose and yelped with the shock.

Grace had known older, wiser exchanges with Beattie and Joyce but with Lillian, perhaps because the two of them were closer in age, she enjoyed a curious mix of playful fun and the willingness to disclose serious matters to her friend.

Today it was Lillian's turn. Numbers at the school would drop at the end of the year, with three older boys finishing and the little ones not yet school age.

'Looks like I'll have to leave Low Head to find suitable work. I'll drop below the quota so they'll cut my pay.'

Grace was dismayed to see her friend so stressed and was cross with herself that she'd been caught up in her own world and hadn't recognised Lillian had issues of her own.

'Surely there's something we can do. There's fifteen families here, give or take. If everyone banded together, maybe we could write to the Department of Education,' was the best response that Grace could make. She was hopeless at this, she thought. Lillian needed more from her friend than a useless plan of attack.

'Good of you to suggest it, Grace, but they're strict about keeping the stipends linked to the numbers.' The resignation in her voice echoed in the room and it spurred Grace on to be more of a friend.

'You don't sound too good, if you'll forgive me saying. Is there something more going on?'

Johnny was hungry and Lillian handed him over for a nappy change and feeding. 'I'm feeling a bit defeated, to be honest, and lacking energy. I've not been myself for a few weeks now.'

Grace recommended she see Doctor Grey, and that going to George Town for a check-up might be helpful. 'He's good, Lillian. He'll know if you're not well or if what's ailing you is to do with the worries you have.'

Lillian seemed unconvinced and they chatted on. Grace was tucking in Johnny for a sleep when her friend went home.

Two days later, she was heading into the Superintendent's laundry to set the fire under the copper when she saw the children crowded at the side of the school, several adults among them, and the doctor's car nearby. The pilot station was strangely silent, despite the size of the gathering.

She left Johnny kicking and gurgling in his pram and ran, full pelt. Halfway down the hill, she saw the mortuary van speeding along the road. Its tyres kicked up dust as it raced through the gate and stopped abruptly near the crowd.

She knew it was Lillian before the stretcher came out the schoolroom door. She pushed through the throng, not noticing who she shoved aside. When she glimpsed the buckle on one of her friend's polished brown shoes, the blanket not entirely concealing it, she lurched to one side and almost slumped to the ground. Around her, several children cried and whimpered.

The Superintendent was shepherding the group away. 'Go home now, we'll meet in the church at seven o'clock and pray for her soul.'

Tommy seized Grace's elbow and gently propped against her until the desire to collapse had passed. 'Where's Johnny, Grace?'

She staggered up the path, his arm around her while she sobbed uncontrollably. She was Lillian's friend but she'd been the last to know she'd died. 'I wasn't there for her. I wasn't there …'

'You couldn't have known, Grace. Nobody did.'

The words were barely from his mouth when she turned suddenly, savagely beating her fists on his chest. 'It's my fault. Mine! You don't understand.' Her hands punched out the end of each sentence. 'She was sick on Sunday and I did nothing. Ignored her. I'm useless, no good for anybody, I'm the one who doesn't deserve to live.'

She thumped at her own chest and then banged her fists hard on the side of her head.

Tommy grabbed her wrists and held them firmly. They were close enough to the Superintendent's cottage to hear Johnny screaming, the pitch getting higher as he worked himself into a state, but Grace was lost in her own rising hysteria.

She let Tommy manhandle her the last twenty yards and manoeuvre her into a chair. Nothing mattered anymore. She knew she should pick up the baby and soothe him but she left Tommy to do it. Years of resistance crashed down and she collapsed at the table, head in her hands, and gave in to grief so deep she could no longer tell what it was for.

Tommy made no attempt to comfort her, not even a squeeze on the shoulder. Whatever journey she was taking, she had to go on her own. He stayed close, saying nothing, walking with the baby in the room, and when Grace's keening distressed the boy, he carried him out the door. Grace saw him point across the grassy lighthouse knoll and show the baby how the river was pouring out into the sea.

Though Tommy spoke softly, she heard the words. 'She's okay, little fellow. Your mum, she's emptying out for now but you'll see, it won't be long till the spring tide comes in.'

It must have been close to six when the Superintendent put his head in the door and immediately withdrew. Grace was still crying but in short spasms by now. She called him back and told him she was going home. Tommy had managed to console Johnny for nearly two hours, but the baby was well past his feed and his fretting had taken on a serious note.

Tommy carried the boy while Grace pushed the pram, glad to have the handle to grip. It made no sense, all that lay before her. The houses in their semi-circle, the hexagonal map room, the pilot station office, the workshops and boatshed, even the schoolroom, looked exactly the same yet Lillian was gone.

Back at her cottage, Tommy got her to eat a piece of bread and jam. A few minutes before seven he made to leave for the church but she insisted on going with him. She left the pram in the kitchen and they took turns carrying the sleepy baby. A few heads turned when they walked in together but all eyes faced front as the lay preacher, one of their own, stood and mothers shushed their tired children.

Christ Church, located opposite the gates of the pilot station, was a workers' chapel, unpretentious despite attempts by whoever designed it to reference enduring symbols of spiritual elevation and light. Three narrow arched windows on either wall and two even narrower stained-glass windows on each side of the porch set limits to the light, Grace thought, pinching it in rather than opening it out.

It was not a formal ceremony, Mr Williams hastened to tell them all. That would come later once the family had made suitable arrangements. They had gathered in the meantime to share their sense of shock and loss — that a fine young teacher and friend of the pilot station had so cruelly departed.

Grace, her mind drained of all thought, hugged Johnny to her and waited for the preacher to read a psalm or two. Instead, he read a Tennyson poem.

Sunset and evening star,
And one clear call for me!

And may there be no moaning of the bar,
When I put out to sea,

But such a tide as moving seems asleep,
Too full for sound and foam,
When that which drew from out the boundless deep
Turns again home.

Twilight and evening bell,
And after that the dark!
And may there be no sadness of farewell,
When I embark;

For through from out our bourne of Time and Place
The flood may bear me far,
I hope to see my Pilot face to face
When I have crossed the bar.

The harmonium remained silent. The congregation had no appetite for singing hymns.

It was fitting, the preacher said, that Miss Munro had chosen to spend her final days in their community, where she was respected and loved; where each day, she could see the river and the ships passing by.

'She knew her time was short and we are privileged that she stayed and gave her talent and energy to furthering the learning of our children.'

At the words, Grace froze. Lillian had not confided any such knowledge in her.

Any sounds from the pews were subdued as the Superintendent rose to address them regarding practical matters. Given the progress of the school year, the department was not in a position to supply a replacement teacher for two weeks, he informed them.

It was proposed that the children would, in the

interim, undertake half days where they would be supervised in practising their reading and writing, as well as undertaking exercises already prepared by Miss Munro. The children would have the day off tomorrow while a roster was drawn up.

As the gathering left for home, few lingered in the cold. The Superintendent was at the edge of the last row of houses and starting uphill when Grace caught up with him.

He looked weary, worn down, but she ignored the wave of sympathy that rose in her and pressed him for what he knew. At first he wasn't forthcoming but it was plain she wouldn't let him go until he shared what Doctor Grey had disclosed.

'She had a hole in her heart, Grace. She understood it would get her in the end but the doctor doubts she'd anticipated it would be this soon.' He patted her arm. 'I'm sorry, lass, I know you two were friends.'

She let him walk away. It had taken its toll on him, on them all, and she wasn't the only one to grieve for Lillian and the losses that her passing had reignited.

She had been intent on finding out the truth, about her past and now, about Lillian; so keen to finish things. She trudged home, where Tommy waited patiently, watching over the baby.

After he'd gone, she stood at the window. Though the tower and its lamps lay in the opposite direction, the ground outside was washed by the rhythmic flashing of the light. Each blast of brightness left in its wake an ever-darkening gloom.

The light held her captive against the sill. She was motionless, her mind still. As the beams endlessly sliced up the night, their pattern was as indisputable as her one thought.

No matter how you arrived there, through striving or denial, getting to the truth would never bring a person to the end of anything.

14

The Superintendent was the last person she expected to see when she opened the door the next morning, her eyes still swollen.

'Mind if I come in for a minute?'

She'd just made a pot of tea but he declined the offer of a cup. He'd spent the night thinking on the situation at the school and had come up with a proposal he hoped she might favour.

'It's best for the children to have some continuity until the new teacher arrives, to keep them in school at least for the mornings. I'll talk to Mrs Jacques and a couple of the others who might be willing, but the kids already know you.'

He would write up a roster to cover the other women taking a turn each day settling the group in class for the first hour or so, and then Grace would take over from half past ten till for a couple of hours.

'It's a bit unorthodox, true, especially when you have the boy, and I'm not denying it'll make some unhappy, you being on your own and all. But they'll see the sense of it and I'm hoping you'll agree to help us out.'

He gave her the schoolhouse key and encouraged her to go in later in the day and check the textbooks and papers Lillian had left on her desk. A reply was evidently unnecessary, as he left without Grace giving him one.

It was mid-afternoon before she could bring herself to finish up at the Superintendent's cottage and go to the school.

At three months old, Johnny was sleeping longer at night and awake more during the day. She dragged the pram into the schoolroom and propped him up with a pillow. She had the teething peg tied to one end of a piece of string and the other tied to the hood of the pram, and he'd taken a liking to swiping at it and mostly missing. He smiled widely and chuckled through bubbles of spit. She laughed with him as she wiped the saliva from his chin.

It helped, as she explored Lillian's schoolroom, that the baby was gurgling and chortling in his play. The children's workbooks were still open on their desks, and on the blackboard, rows of calculations to the left gave examples of complicated fractions for the older students. On the right, Lillian had been teaching the younger ones a simpler way, with a drawing she'd done of a round cake cut in slices.

The teacher's chair was still on its side on the floor where it had tipped as she tried to get to her feet and out the door. Grace sensed the turmoil her friend had been in, aware of her heart giving out, wanting to spare the children the sight of their teacher collapsing, fighting for life.

She straightened the chair and sat at the desk, with its neat piles of books and papers. The timetable for lessons was taped in one corner, and stacked alongside it, in perfect penmanship, were lesson outlines that Lillian didn't have the chance to deliver.

It was overwhelming, the thought of standing in her friend's shoes, but Grace would take it step by step and remain calm and orderly, as Lillian had done. First, she tidied each of the pupils' desks, closing their books and placing them and the discarded pens and pencils neatly in the centre. She cleaned the blackboard and laid out fresh chalk on the ledge.

Mrs Williams would take the children through their reading in the morning. Grace would attempt geography. She had no training, no skills and no confidence, so it wouldn't be a lesson; however, together, she and the children could choose a country or two and have a discussion. Perhaps the older ones could help. She found the geography textbook in Lillian's pile and put it in the pram.

She took the schoolhouse key to Mrs Williams, whose husband was a leading boatman when he wasn't taking a turn at the pulpit. The woman was unexpectedly eager to supervise the children, telling Grace she'd been an exemplary student and pupil teacher in her day, at thirteen years old often in charge of forty children at her country school. 'You need to show them your authority. It's all about a firm hand.'

Grace smiled to herself on the way home. By the time Mrs Williams had finished her session, the pupils would be relieved to have a friendly face in the classroom.

Not for a moment did Grace see herself as a teacher but as the days went by, she found her feet with the children and they had spirited discussions about history, nature, books they were reading, and the world at large. She prepared a list of the ships that plied the river outside their door and they tracked their voyages to ports in Australia and overseas, studied their cargos and economic contribution, and explored what it would be like for sailors to leave their country for years at a time.

She spent the afternoons cleaning and cooking for the Superintendent and in the evenings, Johnny balanced on one knee, worked her way through Lillian's textbooks. Sometimes, in the middle of a session when a child asked a question that she couldn't answer, she would pull out one of the books. 'Let's see if we can find out together.'

Occasionally, Mrs Jacques took Johnny for the two hours but mostly he went to the schoolroom. The older girls were happy to take a turn holding him when he'd had enough of the pram or she'd lay a blanket down for him in the corner, where he could practise his attempts at rolling over.

Lillian's funeral on the Friday was in Hobart, which meant the Low Head folk wouldn't be able to attend. The Superintendent drove south to represent them all.

The service was scheduled for half past eleven and when the schoolroom clock reached the half hour, Grace asked everyone to close their books, bow their heads and observe a minute's silence for their teacher. Afterwards, it seemed wrong to simply go on with the lesson so she gave them a chance to say what they'd most learnt from Miss Munro.

It was Ruby who brought her to tears. 'Miss Munro showed me that it's okay to be kind, even when you know someone is wrong.'

Tommy dropped by briefly in the evenings but with so much to do, she didn't encourage him to stay.

The first time she showed him to the door to leave, he protested, saying he wanted to spend more time with her and the baby, but she wasn't swayed. 'I need to do the best I can at the school, not for the parents or even the kids, but for Lillian and especially for me.'

By the end of the week, he was angry at being pushed away. She didn't know why but she began telling him about the bird she'd seen, not long after arriving at the pilot station, a sea eagle in a tree above East Beach. As she'd approached, it had taken to the air, heavy-bellied, its wings labouring with the effort to lift off.

Tommy had a puzzled expression on his face when he left, for she hadn't been able to finish the story.

She couldn't bring herself to say it until he'd gone and there was only the baby to hear. 'Don't tell a soul, little one, or they'll think I've gone mad. It's like I'm that bird, weighed down and giving it all I've got and maybe, just maybe, slowly rising.'

She was sad when the second week came to an end and she had to leave the textbooks on the desk. They all gathered in the church on Sunday evening to welcome the new teacher, an older widow who couldn't have been more different to Miss Munro. The Superintendent was profuse in his thanks to Grace and the other three women in tiding the children over.

Reluctantly, Grace returned to her routine. She knew she'd hurt Tommy, and many times she told herself that she should go and knock on his door, apologise for her behaviour, but it wasn't right to do so.

If Joyce, or anyone for that matter, had dared to ask why not, she might have concocted an answer because there should have been one. That she didn't deserve him? That he would have a better future with someone else? That it wasn't fair for him to raise a child not his own?

In reality, she had no explanation. She was not a woman who'd have a better chance to marry, if that was indeed what Tommy might suggest. Plenty of unwed women with a child would never get a decent man.

She'd grown fond of Tommy, which made it more of

a mystery that she should turn away someone who was kind to her and brave enough to care for a baby who was not his own and worse, had come into the world in such a dire way. It plagued her, especially at night when she had no tasks for diversion, that Tommy had been steady and the circumstances settled yet her instincts wouldn't let her go to him.

Since the day she'd caught the ferry from the rescue home, she'd been tested at every turn. She'd gone down unfamiliar tracks and once or twice, lost the path completely; however, each time, coming to meet her, had been a new version of herself.

This stubbornness with Tommy was different, but she didn't know how. She was at the mercy of a determined self that refused to make itself known.

The new teacher had no need for assistance — 'I'm quite capable, thank you' — and Grace spent her days tending to the baby and the Superintendent's cottage, washing and meals. At night she dreamed of digging a deep hole in bright daylight, and then after dark, shoveling all the damp earth back in before the sun came up so it was ready to empty again.

She began to wish, when she woke, that she could climb into the hole and cover herself with the moist-smelling soil.

With Lillian gone and Tommy no longer visiting, she leaned a little more on Joyce for company, though what conversation they shared was generally limited to children and domestic matters. She needed the human connection but increasingly the visits left her drained.

Though spring was well under way, there'd been a cold snap and she was wrestling Johnny to get a knitted cap on his head before leaving the Jacques' cottage one afternoon. The question burst from her, unbidden. 'You always seem so settled. Do you ever wish for more, Joyce?'

Her friend snapped her head to the side and glanced at the ceiling, quickly, as though ducking a missile. Grace held the baby up for his goodbye kiss, without expecting an answer, when Joyce replied, 'What woman doesn't? Sure, when I was young I dreamed of having my own income and a job, maybe my own place. Then you marry and the kids come along and all you wish for is a day to yourself and maybe an outing once a year to the picture theatre.'

She paused, eyes down. 'You're young, Grace, so you have to trust me when I say that it's not what you wish for that matters. You'll find that the trick to having a satisfying life is to know what to give and when to give it.'

It was a point worth arguing, Grace thought, but Johnny was tired and short-tempered and she needed to get him home. Hurrying off with the complaining baby, she thought it had been a close call. If she hadn't needed to leave she'd have been snappy with Joyce, because if life was about giving then she ought, by rights, be very bloody happy indeed.

Perhaps Joyce was seeing it from the wrong side, that contentment was about receiving, but that made no sense either when Tommy was making it plain he was ready to give and she couldn't let herself take what he offered. It made her head hurt, trying to smooth out the kinks in her thinking. She should just get on with it, like other women did.

She couldn't tell Joyce that secretly she wondered if she was flawed like her father, that sometimes she examined her mind, searching for weak spots where the ground might give way. Then what would become of Johnny, dependent on a woman with a foundation that needed pinning?

During the two weeks in Lillian's classroom, dare she say it, she'd shown herself capable, had stretched old boundaries through learning and a willingness to try the new. It had been a form of flight, opening up the view. The life before had momentarily fallen away. She'd seen from a distance the woman she'd been: poor, sad Grace Anderson — damaged, neglected, used, abused. And she didn't want that woman on her back.

In the night an unseasonal northwesterly gale blew up, much stronger than had been predicted. Grace heard the rain hammering on the roof through the night and groggy with sleep, she thought she heard shouts but couldn't rouse herself sufficiently to go outside and check.

The storm passed at first light and soon after she heard men calling to each other. From her front door she saw the sea had been carried in on the night tide, whipped along by the wind, and had flooded the jetty and low grounds of the pilot station and knocked out a section of post and rail fence.

Two boatmen were calling to each other as they attempted to retrieve a dinghy, torn away along with davits that secured it to the jetty and dragged over rocks in Lagoon Bay. A few others were bellowing about a recovery mission for the black buoy that usually marked the middle ground but had been wrenched from its moorings. Until the water level dropped and the jetty could be accessed, it would be left floating in the river.

Grace closed the door and went to change Johnny's nappy because she couldn't bear the thought that like the marker buoy, she'd been left to drift.

WEEKS PASSED FOR Grace in a haze of work and mothering. Doctor Grey had been making a house call, stitching a leg wound one of the pilots had sustained with a grappling hook. Sleeves rolled up to beat the heat of the summer's day, he took the opportunity to call on Grace at the Superintendent's cottage and check on Johnny's health and progress.

Even inside the cottage it was hard to escape the sharp dung smell of the nearby penguin colony. Hundreds of the little birds had made their way back from sea to old burrows under the boxthorn bushes below the lighthouse. It was their season for mating and moulting. Some had settled in under the Jacques' bedroom and Joyce had been complaining for days that the early morning rumbling and trumpeting was driving her nuts.

The doctor listened to Johnny's heart and lungs with a stethoscope, checked the movement of limbs, tested his reflexes and measured his length before declaring the five-month-old in fine form. 'You've done really well. He's in perfect health and thriving. What about you?'

The inquiry was blunt, it had none of the doctor's usual tact, and if the intention had been to ambush Grace into an honest response, it failed to work.

'He's a happy boy and brings me more joy than I'd ever imagined was possible.'

The doctor lowered his glasses to the tip of his nose and looked at her over the top of them. Undeterred, he took a more confessional tone. 'It's all right, lass, to be honest with me. I can see you're managing just fine and I have no complaint about the way you care for the baby. But you're heavy-hearted and I'm wondering why.'

It spilled out then, she had no ability to stop it, what

she'd learnt from the Superintendent and the yellow pieces of paper in the bottom of his trunk, the terror and the pain that latched on from that August night. She'd said more than she'd wanted to and she tried to call a halt but the stream of thoughts kept rushing out her mouth. How she'd talked to the Superintendent that difficult day and discovered more about her father than perhaps she was equipped to know.

Doctor Grey listened, letting every word flow without comment or advice until the flood had passed, and then he asked for a cup of tea.

They sat in silence, broken only by the sound of the boiling kettle.

The doctor waited to speak until Grace was busy warming the pot and gathering the cups and saucers. 'In my line of work, I see people in situations that'd curdle milk. We can never know how the human spirit will deal with the challenges God sends. There's nothing I can say about your father, except that he no doubt did his best. My concern lies with you, Grace. When someone breaks an arm, we can all look at the bone and see what the problem is. If all we had to go on was our imagination, who knows what we might conclude?'

He counselled her to have a kinder regard for herself. She was trying to come to terms with a peculiar situation. 'You lost your father at an early age, but in finding him, he's slipped away again.'

It wasn't so much what the doctor said, she thought later in the day, but his straightforward tone. She wasn't going mad after all. In trying to reconcile a father neither truly alive nor lying in his grave, her mind had lost its logic and the compass in her heart pointed every direction and none.

Later, on the walk home, she had the strange sensation of being chased. She looked back and the path was empty but the feeling of something on her tail persisted and she picked up the pace. As she strode along, the realisation caught up. She felt it as a wave of heat travelling up her legs and trunk to her throat.

She recognised what it required her to do.

At half past eight the next morning, she knocked on the office door and asked the Superintendent if she could use the telephone.

15

The rocking of the train suited Johnny and he slept in her arms or on the seat beside her for much of the trip. At the tunnel, she wordlessly congratulated the younger girl who'd headed north at the beginning of the year, in touch with her ignorance but unaware of any skerrick of courage within.

She'd had no cause in recent months to spend her wages beyond rent, food and what the baby needed and had several pound notes from her savings tucked in her purse. The Superintendent had gladly agreed to her taking the Thursday and Friday off, saying he wasn't sure the trip was a good thing but he understood the need for it.

Tommy had been less forthcoming when she told him about going away for a couple of days. 'You have to do what you must, Grace,' was all that he'd said. Johnny had waved a hand towards him as though waiting for his usual squeeze but was disappointed, too, when Tommy walked off.

It was late afternoon when they pulled into the station and Grace was overcome by the noise and activity on the platform and the buzz of a city gearing up for Christmas. The guard retrieved the pram from the side of the luggage car before unloading suitcases and bags stacked high. With the crowd shoving in, Johnny began to cry and she thought of the calm and quiet of her little home, with the sun going down and the tower bracing itself to hold back the night.

She'd booked a guesthouse close to the railway station as 'Mrs' Anderson, though didn't attempt to complete the ruse through the purchase of a wedding ring. By the time she arrived, Johnny was kicking up a fuss and she gladly agreed to take her meal on a tray in her room.

Despite a long feed, he proved difficult to settle and she wondered if it was the strange cot, not thinking he might be reacting to the anxiety engulfing her since they'd arrived at the station.

Next morning the Astor Motor Service coach didn't leave until eleven, which gave Grace time to shop for a small gift. The guesthouse proprietor waited in the hall as Grace carried Johnny downstairs to his pram. The woman may have been attractive once, though it was hard to tell under the makeup that clumped in lines and crevices across her face. She looked at the baby while addressing Grace. 'You'll be wanting a tray again tonight?'

Grace nodded and left as quickly as she could, glad to have the freedom of the pavement and the distraction of bright colours in Christmas displays strung across shop windows.

She explored merchandise at three stores, glancing over cufflinks, toiletries, striped neckties, dress socks and razor kits, ruling them out as fast as she sighted them. Nothing seemed right. The clock was ticking down and a sick desperation made it hard to think. In the end she opted for a safe choice, a shoe cleaning kit in a smart wooden box.

The bus stop was outside the Palace Theatre, where she kept her eyes fixed on traffic in Elizabeth Street so she didn't have to look up the stairs towards the cavern of the theatre foyer. Knowing it was at her back was discomforting. Though the morning was cool, she began to sweat, waiting until a group of businessmen had passed before scratching at the damp armpits of her blue dress.

She rolled the pram back and forth, hoping to keep Johnny settled. It had been nerve-wracking feeding him on the train, using a shawl for privacy, but she would have to offer him the breast on the bus, and in such close confines that could be more difficult.

She took out her handkerchief and wiped Johnny's mouth. It was barely back in her handbag before she took it out and wiped his cheek again. She tucked his blanket firmly under his arms though he was wriggling wildly with the effort of trying to sit up. Thwarted, he let out a sharp wail and she hastily lifted him into her arms to soothe his cries.

He squirmed on her hip, throwing his chest from side to side and shaking his head. For an absurd moment, she thought she might join him in a temper tantrum right there in the street, flinging her arms and legs about to discharge the ragged tension in her chest. As though hearing her thoughts, Johnny immediately started a low-key whine.

Just when she thought she couldn't stay upright for a minute more, the bus pulled in at the kerb. The pulsing roar of the motor brought Johnny's distress to a rapid stop and he stared in wonder at the coach, remaining quiet while the driver folded down the handle on the pram and loaded it in the back. She took a seat towards the rear and was relieved when the coach accelerated away from the stop.

They followed the river in the same direction she'd taken on the train months earlier, except this time she saw facades of retail stores and front doors of houses instead of alleyways and backyards. Johnny, on her knee, was content to watch along with her.

Shopfronts glided by until North Hobart, where grand double verandahs trimmed with lacework dominated the streetscape. The outlook opened out at New Town and she could see the remains of orchards and market gardens, where housing subdivisions were eating their way uphill into what had been wide spaces.

On the right, new weatherboard homes clustered close to the zincworks on the riverbank, where grey plumes rose steadily from smokestacks and powdery residue coated the manufacturing plant.

At Bridgewater, while the train track veered north across the causeway and away from the river, the road continued to cling to the water's edge. The spreading reach of the Derwent was covered in black swans, a hundred or more. Some drifted across the water, others plunged long necks into weeds for food or in the shallows at the river edge.

As the bus drew level with a pair, they lifted off as one, necks stretched forward, flying low. Grace's anxiety was dislodged temporarily by amazement at the brilliant white flash underneath the wide wings, before the swans gained height and the bus left them behind.

Approaching the outskirts of New Norfolk, a series of dreary brick buildings were visible, grouped together at a distance. A high, brick wall ran along two sides and towering above it was a double-story structure with a clock tower. Grace was the child of an institution and she didn't need anyone to tell her she was looking at the asylum.

The bus stopped in the town's main street and Grace waited until all the passengers had collected their luggage and dispersed before asking the driver for directions to the Mental Diseases Hospital. If he was curious about why a young woman would take a child to the asylum, he covered it up and spared her the embarrassment of any difficult questions.

The town stretched along two sides of the hospital compound, which meant that she and Johnny were only three or four streets away. The driver gave instructions for the route to the wall and The Avenue, telling her the entrance was quite some way along it. She calculated that she'd need twenty minutes to get there and with more than an hour to spare, went looking for a café.

Johnny squirmed in the pram, despite being recently fed and due for a nap. He whined unhappily, kicking off his blanket and causing Grace to wonder if he was protesting at the purpose of their trip.

As she pushed the pram down High Street, her own doubts flooded in. The sensible thing would be to accept she'd made an error of judgment and salvage some pleasure from the day by walking down to the river and doing some exploring until the bus was due to leave. It made sense to change her plans and it was nobody's business if that was the case.

She parked the pram in the street and carried Johnny into a café, where she took a booth so she could lay the baby beside her on the bench, one hand scooping him close to stop him rolling off.

She lingered over the curried egg sandwich and strong black tea, watching the baby as his eyelids grew heavy and then closed. As Johnny surrendered to sleep, she gave in to the powerful grip of panic. *Enough. You have the baby. He's all the family you need.*

She paid the waitress and took Johnny out to the pram,

going down the street with the determination to admire the gardens in nearby Arthur Square, and then make her way to The Esplanade along the river. At least she'd have some enjoyment to make up for the waste of the trip.

She was almost at the entrance to the gardens when, with an impulse that caught her by surprise, she swung into a street on her right and back around the block, going at a rapid pace until she reached The Avenue. Slowing, she continued towards the hospital gatehouse, aware only of the propulsion of her limbs and the flash of metal railings on the hospital's front fence.

The attendant at the gatehouse remained behind his narrow desk as he gestured for her to sign in, showing no interest in the pram. He pointed in the direction of the visitors room and left her to find her way.

Her face flushed hot and prickled despite a cool wind coming up from the river. The pram wheels rumbled in the loose gravel on the path, loudly reinforcing the shuddering in her chest. She recognised, too late, that the motivation for making the trip had been a sense of possibility and that whoever waited in the room ahead couldn't hope to shoulder such a burden.

She followed the sign to the male asylum, a double-storey brick building squatting heavily on the edge of lawn. The sloping roofing iron on the full-length verandah cast dark shadows onto the building. Daisy bushes and a few haphazard, straggly roses grew in a couple of garden beds that seemed to have been randomly tossed in the grass.

Inside the entrance, another attendant, a short man with an unruly moustache, showed her into the visitors room and left to fetch Jack Anderson.

Each wall of the room had windows from the halfway

mark to the ceiling. Rows of metal-framed chairs with straight backs were pushed against two sides, their outline stark under the bright artificial lighting. Grace was accustomed to strong smells: the tang of seaweed, freshness of dew-covered grass, meat cooking slowly in a stew. The absence of any smells in the room bothered her, not even a whiff of disinfectant.

The attendant stepped lively in the corridor, past the row of internal windows, heading in Grace's direction. Behind him lagged a man whose shoulders and head were stiff, locked together at the neck. When he entered the room, Grace stood and instinctively met his eyes. They were soft grey and searching, focused not on her face but the surrounding space. The eyes inhabited their own zone, out of kilter with the thin lips and slack jaw.

The attendant gestured for his charge to take a seat and left the room, returning to his desk in the corridor. Grace sat one chair along from Jack, lifting Johnny from the pram and holding him on her lap. The three of them sat in silence, even the baby unable to muster a sound.

It was Jack who spoke first, pausing to breathe heavily after every few words.

'Amy, I always knew you'd come. And look, you've brought Grace.' Jack smiled then. He didn't reach out to touch them but wrapped his arms around his chest, hugging himself tight.

As though keen to assert his own identity, Johnny arched his back, opened his mouth and let out a long wail. As Grace comforted him, she searched the face of the stranger opposite for any familiar contour or mark. She saw nothing of her own features, though Johnny shared elongated ear lobes similar to the man before her. Or maybe it was her imagination spinning a quick story to establish a pretence of connection.

All Grace wanted in that moment was to be in her cottage with Johnny and know the door was shut tight. The man who was supposedly her father was no fantasy. He sat in front of her, a confounding parcel of flesh and blood, and she had no wish to explain who she really was. For the second time that day, the only desire she had was to be wandering carefree along the river.

It was hard to tell how long she stayed. It may have been as long as an hour though it was possibly mere minutes. Neither she nor the stranger had much to offer by way of conversation.

She attempted to explain that she was Grace and this was his grandson, Johnny. It was the right thing to do.

She thought to ease any concern of his about how much she understood, to indicate that she knew about her mother and brother drowning, the terrible sorrow of it for him, and that she now lived at Low Head as he had done. However, her throat remained closed.

He gave no acknowledgement of what little she said.

When she rose to settle Johnny back in the pram, the attendant returned. 'Come on, Jack, we'll take you back to the day room.'

As he stood, body rigid, a confused look passed over his face before it turned to fear. He looked to Grace for what she immediately recognised as a need for reassurance.

'It's okay, Jack. We'll come back and see you another time.' She remembered the gift and held it towards him. He didn't seem to know what to do with the parcel. It hung from her hand in the air between them, meaningless as the visit itself. 'It's for you. Perhaps you'll find it useful.'

He continued to look at it without reaction. The attendant took the parcel and placed it against Jack's chest, and with the contact, Jack's arms came up and he cradled the gift to him. He nodded just once and followed the attendant out.

Grace was still rooted to the spot when the attendant returned ten minutes later, feeling the need to tell her that he'd checked the gift to make sure it contained no sharp objects, alcohol or valuables. It was fine and they'd let Jack keep it.

She made no move to leave. When he attempted to show her out she told him it was impossible to depart without gaining an understanding of her father's condition.

'Sorry love. I'm not supposed to give that kind of information. You'll have to book an appointment to see the Matron.'

It may have been the desperation in her voice when she explained about the long trip from home and the possibility she may only ever get to visit once, but after glancing around to see no other staff were nearby, he relented.

In a semi-whisper, he told her that Jack Anderson for the first few years had been a refractory patient, requiring constant supervision and containment for behaviour that was often out of control. 'He's never going to be cured or be able to look after himself, of course, but now he's no threat. They let him walk in the grounds but he doesn't like going far. He can do a bit of manual work, as long as it's straightforward. That's about it.' The attendant looked over his shoulder after he spoke, wary that he might be seen talking with her, but she wasn't giving up just yet.

'What's it like in here?'

The man shook his head to prevent further questions

and turned towards the door, as if to return to his station.

'Please, please tell me. It's taken me years to find him, I need to know.'

He hesitated briefly. A woman's voice could be heard from the verandah, and then it faded away. 'It's not for me to say. I've got a wife and four kids, I need the job.'

Grace pulled the pram in so tight the handle dug into her waist. 'I'm not aiming to make trouble. You're a father so you'll understand I'm just trying to fathom things as family.'

He smoothed his moustache down so firmly the corners of his top lip were stretched towards his chin.

The corridor remained silent.

His awkwardness made it clear he was getting desperate for her to leave. 'I guess there's a chance you read the Hobart paper last month and saw the account of the hospital's annual report when it was tabled in Parliament? So you wouldn't need me to tell you this place is overcrowded, they can't keep the nurses, and the buildings are going to rack and ruin. The only way many of 'em leave is in a box and that's a blessed relief for some, though the report reckoned the average age at fifty-four.' He pushed his face in close towards hers. 'You didn't hear any of that from me.' He insisted then that Grace go so he could return to his desk.

Halfway along The Avenue, a passerby gave Grace a strange look and she realised she was running in long strides with the pram. She forced herself to slow to a more suitable pace, but without the exertion, all she saw was Jack Anderson holding the gift to himself and turning away.

Grace reached the bus stop way too early but could think of nowhere else to go. She stayed put and rocked the pram, a useless task as Johnny was already asleep.

She hadn't known what to expect from the visit but now her father seemed more dead to her than before and she had no idea how to feel about that.

16

Two days had passed since Grace had returned to Low Head and still she hadn't seen Tommy around the pilot station. Joyce dropped in at the Superintendent's cottage late on the third morning, showing her usual restraint though Grace could tell she was curious about the trip south.

She told Joyce about the visit, sticking to the facts and providing little description of the man she had finally faced. If Joyce was surprised by any of what was shared, it didn't show in her expression. All that needed to be said was in the brief squeeze of her hand when she reached over with one broad palm, before they moved on to other matters.

The two women chatted companionably, taking turns to provide updates on children, domestic routines, practical matters. The predictable pattern of the conversation was comforting to Grace — a consoling rhythm of skinned knees, washing days, snail damage in the fledgling cabbage plants, and errors with the grocery delivery.

It was a relief for daily demands to be so thoroughly restored and Grace felt the tension she'd carried begin to ease.

Joyce was almost out the door before Grace inquired about Tommy.

'Oh, didn't you know? He's had to go back to the farm, poor fellow. His father had been rounding up sheep and collapsed. They think it was a stroke. His foot was hooked in the stirrup and the horse dragged him the length of the paddock before it was caught.'

Grace was holding the door open as Joyce got to the end of the sentence. She leaned heavily on its handle, hoping Joyce wouldn't notice. 'That's shocking. A terrible thing. How long's he likely to be gone?'

'No one knows. His dad was pretty knocked around so depends on how he goes and what help the brother needs on the farm, I expect.' Joyce turned to go, then looked back over her shoulder. 'Meant to say before you left, you and Johnny are more than welcome to have Christmas dinner with us if you think the roast pork'll compensate for the racket my mob make. Alf's coming too.'

Mid-afternoon, Grace was changing Johnny out of a woollen vest that he had soiled along with his nappy. Distracted, she pulled his hand back more sharply than she'd intended and must have hurt the boy for he let out a shriek and tears ran down the curve of his round cheek.

She was angry with herself, but by the time she had leaned over to soothe the baby, her own tears were falling and mingling with his. She scooped him up to her chest and rocked him there until he quieted, the whole time her shoulders shaking with the effort of holding back what was building within.

They left the Superintendent's cottage soon afterwards. Despite the gentle downhill gradient of the path to her house, the act of pushing the pram home was exhausting. She was glad when she bundled Johnny through the back door.

It might have been the tiredness but she had the distinct sense she wasn't aging in accordance with the calendar but to the ever-faster ticking of a clock. Like someone had wound the pendulum too tight and the wheels and cogs might give at any moment.

She looked in the mirror, half expecting to see a wrinkled face look back but it was the same Grace she'd seen when brushing her hair that morning. *Is this how it starts, the going mad?*

The baby wriggled and squirmed on her hip. *Take it easy. Be the mother he needs.* She settled on a chair and began feeding him but couldn't shake the feeling she had come to the edge, and one way or another, she was going over.

'What's happening, Johnny?' she whispered in his ear.

The silence that followed was more than she could bear so she began singing the nursery rhymes Mary had once sung to her. They filled the space and seemed to entertain the baby as he suckled, but they did nothing to comfort her.

If her mother had lived, everything would have been different. She would have been given succour and emotional security. She would have had a father nearby with all the protection he could provide. How she had yearned for what he could give, the hazy father who had sent money from across a great divide. He didn't have the expressionless face of Jack Anderson. She could not reconcile the two.

She continued singing to Johnny even when he had fallen asleep on her lap. Below the tunes and the childish rhymes, her thoughts remained undisciplined. Scraps of disconnected ideas or maybe memories — she could no longer tell — were flinging themselves at the blank wall she had thrown up years ago, when the police hauled Mary away.

Tommy had been right about that wall and she so badly wanted to talk to him but refused to allow herself that notion or the sadness she felt at the distress her friend would be experiencing on the family farm. He seemed as remote as the man she'd visited at New Norfolk.

Twilight had almost given in to night when she stirred and put Johnny to bed. She sliced a cold beef sausage and ate it on a piece of bread she didn't bother to butter, with the intention of turning in early. It transpired that she was far too tired to sleep, her body unwilling to bend into the hollow of the mattress. She threw back the covers and sprang up, setting about wrapping the modest Christmas presents she'd bought on the last morning in Hobart.

Christmas Day dawned windy and cloudy. She'd sewn a red stocking for Johnny's Santa present and placed a wind-up tin dog in it the night before. The boy stared wide-eyed when she turned the key several times and let the stiff legs click their way across the table.

She'd made mince pies before the New Norfolk trip and at midday packed a dozen in her basket to share at Joyce's. It was hard to know what to expect of the gathering, where she would be neither a charity case nor a servant, both of which necessitated the expression of overwhelming gratitude for the slightest kindness. To attend as a guest and friend would be something else altogether. Now the time approached, she was a little nervous.

Striding up the hill, she heard children's shouts well in advance of the Jacques' cottage. The older two boys had received a cricket set and were putting it to good use, with loud dissent over the rules and bellowing at the younger kids in a vain attempt to get them to stick to their positions in the outfield.

Will Jacques watched his brood with amusement, pipe in mouth, from a bench on the sheltered side of their cottage. 'Merry Christmas to you, Grace,' he called as she approached. 'Leave Johnny here with me if you want and I'll entertain him while you give Joyce a hand. I know she'd be glad of it!'

Inside, Joyce was commanding pots on the stove, expertly adjusting their positions to even up the cooking times while maintaining a grip on the folded tea towel protecting her palm. Her face was almost the same shade and shine as the pork when she pulled it out of the oven.

'Shame we can't open the windows and the door but it'll only be an invitation to the blowflies. Glad you're here, Grace, I'll get you to finish off the apple sauce.'

The Superintendent turned up a half hour later, just as the roast potatoes had finished crisping and Joyce was declaring that all was ready.

It was not a day for formalities, evidently. 'Make yourself useful, Alf — mix Grace and me a shandy, would you? And pour yourself a beer.'

Will Jacques followed his boss in the door, with a grin. 'Well, Superintendent sir, seems Joyce is the one giving the orders today.'

With that, his wife sent him back outside to round up the kids.

After all the quiet conversations she'd had with Joyce in this kitchen since her arrival, the noise and chaos was a shock for Grace as everyone squeezed around the table, elbows in and dinner plates almost touching.

There was a momentary ceasefire as they all crossed arms and held hands while Mr Jacques mumbled a hasty grace. The minute the amen had passed everyone's lips the three boys had their forks loaded and on their way to gaping mouths.

The burst of sustained sound that followed could

hardly be called conversation, though there was plenty of talking above the scrape of knives on china and the kids nudging and teasing each other while working their way through their mother's generous helpings.

Grace had Johnny propped on her lap, one arm around him while she attempted to cut the meat, roast pumpkin and spuds with the other hand. When the oldest girl, Coralie, had finished her meal she took Johnny and expertly wedged him on her hip, sweeping him off to show him the cottage features and the Christmas presents. She returned with the baby as Grace finished eating and Joyce took him while Grace sat back in her chair and finished her shandy.

At first she thought it was the alcohol. Through the busy hum, her body was loosening, as though a stream of warm honey was flowing from her crown, sweeping along her shoulders and down her arms. The soothing effect continued long after the drink was gone, as she helped Joyce unwrap the hot Christmas pudding and push in threepences and sixpences for the children to find in their serve.

After the pudding and custard, Grace brought out the mince pies and Joyce made a pot of tea while the men continued with their beer. Joyce had presents for the guests — handknitted socks for the Superintendent, a pot of Yardley's lavender cold cream for Grace, and red felt mittens for Johnny.

Grace in turn handed out gifts of books to the children: Doctor Dolittle for the boys, *The Magical Land of Noom* for Coralie, and for the youngest girl, the latest Gumnut Babies book from May Gibbs.

'That's most generous, Grace. You shouldn't have,' Joyce chided later, after the children had scattered outside with the men following close behind them. Johnny was being entertained by Coralie and the women were working on the first load of dirty dishes.

'I didn't have to, Joyce. It's what you do for family and you've been like family to me.' It seemed like a kind thing to say to her friend but once the sentence was out she knew she meant every word. Without realising it, and with considerable resistance, she had fashioned herself a sort of family that included Joyce, Alf Sturdy, and for a time, Tommy.

It was lumpy and odd, nothing like other families she'd envied or the one she had so often wished for. Yet she'd made her way to it with no obligation to do so. Without the burden of expectation, she could accept it freely. Perhaps families were not about blood kin or grievances that couldn't be healed but were about who was willing to hold your hand, to be by your side when you needed it the most. If that was the case, she most certainly had found a family.

But in all her reckoning about family, the tall, stiff man she'd met at the Mental Diseases Hospital could not be accounted for. He remained a shadow she caught sometimes out the corner of her eye, a trick of the light — best forgotten.

It was late afternoon when she and Alf made their farewells. Johnny was grizzly after all the sounds and motion of the day, having barely slept, but his strained cries ceased immediately when they began walking.

'So you met Jack, then?'

The directness of the question caught Grace unawares. It was unlike Alf to tackle a subject head on, and she wasn't sure what he might be trying to find out. 'I did,' was all she said.

They walked for a few minutes before Alf tried again. 'How is he?'

'I can't rightly say. He didn't talk or give any indication.'

Silence again.

Grace glanced sideways at Alf, who was staring straight ahead.

When he turned to meet her look, his eyes seemed soft but the lines around his mouth were tight. 'Life's not easy, girl. I think you already know that. You can either break down or break open. Some folks, like your dad, don't get much of a choice.' With that, he looked away.

Grace didn't reply, she knew the man by now and understood it was not a subject open to further discussion but Alf's way of offering support.

What he'd said was actually no help at all, she concluded late that evening as she sat by the fire, with Johnny dozing after a bath. It had been an easy enough sentiment for Alf to adopt when he'd survived each round of grief from the death of his babies and his wife.

His trials had been fenced in by a clear beginning and an end. Hers kept scattering, spreading this way and that, growing ever larger while she grew smaller, less able to round up any of it. Choice was a fine thing if you knew what you were up against. It was no match, though, for ghostly imaginings, for a mother who'd died before she'd had the chance to live in your heart, or a father who lived but was the walking dead.

There was only one thing for it. For her sake and Johnny's she must stop thinking about the whole mess.

By New Year's Day, she had largely succeeded and though her energy was flat, at least she was free of the turmoil.

The following Sunday, with time on her hands because it was the one day a week when Alf took care of his own food and cleaning, she set off with the baby for a walk onto the jetty. She stood for a long time, watching the river wend its way peacefully inland with no hint of the dangers that awaited at the mouth or the hidden traps at every turn of the complicated navigation channel.

It could be a beast, ready at any moment to rage or lunge at anything in its path, yet today it was slow and calm. She felt its strength and the way it endured while generations of men and women came and went.

'It'll see me out,' she said to Johnny. 'And you, too.'

As she walked back along the pier, she almost missed the familiar figure of Tommy heading towards his quarters, a rucksack over one shoulder. She waved but he gave no response so she assumed he hadn't seen them.

Unnerved by the sighting, she took Johnny home and paced in front of the stove, twisting and turning back and forth like the river was in her and it was at its worst. Four steps one way, then four back, faster and faster, skirt flying on the turns, and now it wasn't a river but a marksman on her tail and zigzagging was the only way to avoid getting shot.

'For God's sake, Grace. Sit down.'

She had crossed the line, was hearing voices now, giving herself orders in a masculine tone. A stab of panic caught her under the ribs, for what would become of the baby.

As she swung around, she saw the door was open and Tommy was standing on the step.

'You're looking like a madwoman. Whatever has disturbed you so?'

He didn't wait for an answer but pulled out a chair and

dragged it alongside her. She fell onto it, clutching the startled Johnny.

Tommy pressed on with barely a pause. 'I know we didn't part on friendly terms before, Grace, but a lot has happened for you and me since.'

She nodded several times.

'I don't have long. My brother Dave's picking me up soon with my gear.'

Before he could go any further, she burst into his flow of words. 'Tommy, I'm so sorry to hear about your dad. I haven't contacted you about it and it's not because I'm hard-hearted, it's just that I didn't really know where to start. It must be really hard for you and your family ——'

He cut her off then. 'That's the thing, Grace. He's never going to recover, that much is clear. The doctor doesn't know if it was the stroke or the head injury, but other than breathing and taking a little soup or tea now and then, he's not up to doing anything. I've talked it over with my mum and Dave and my sisters and we all agree it's best I go back to the farm. It's only going to be a matter of time and it'll be mine and Dave's anyhow. I always knew this would come, that Dad would be unable to work and I'd be going back, but I guess I thought it'd be further down the track.'

His nose and cheeks were red from windburn and Grace could see he'd lost weight. He looked more like a man of the land than one who'd kept a maritime community in working order.

Sadness was in his eyes, in every move he made. It was in the slump of his shoulders as he reached out to take Johnny in his arms. 'Missed you, little fella.' He bounced the baby gently and Johnny flung a plump arm up and tugged on Tommy's lip.

Grace hadn't budged in the chair. In years to come, she thought, she'd look back on this moment and wonder why the hell she hadn't spoken up, hadn't let a torrent of words loose and be damned about the outcome. Why she didn't reassure Tommy about how much his friendship mattered to her and Johnny. Come from a wilder place than this woman who sat like a river stone.

It was Tommy who did the talking.

'I'm watching my dad die, Grace. It changes you. Time's not a forever thing for me now, and a life, well it's got to be lived with more purpose than the one I had here. I can't be laying there like Dad, coming to my final days and wondering why I was stubborn, why I let pride get in the way.'

She raised her eyes to his.

'I'm only going to say this once, Grace. One shot at getting over myself to speak honestly. I've made it pretty clear that I'm fond of you and Johnny.'

She found some words finally, wooden as they were. 'Oh Tommy, I value our friendship too!'

He was still winding up. 'This isn't about friendship, Grace. I want you to be my wife and for you and Johnny to live with me on the farm. Like I tried to say a while back, it was never going to be an option to do that here. Dave and I plan to build a house for me near the long paddock, and besides, I'm not talking about straight away, I know there's a bit to organise first. But that's what I want and I'm hoping you want that too.'

A wife. She was struggling to see what that had to do with a messed-up woman and her bastard son.

Tommy had stopped now and was waiting for her to respond.

'You know what people will think of you. I expect your family will think the same, Tommy.' She didn't know why she couldn't say yes, why she said such things when she knew they'd hurt.

She'd wounded him. It was in the hard edge of his voice. 'I don't know why you're thinking that way Grace, when you know who I am. You know I'm not one to worry about the neighbours or anyone else.'

She softened for a moment. 'I care about you, Tommy. I really do.' She didn't need him to say it. She could hear it for herself. She was stuck in the same loop as the last time he'd broached the subject.

Except this round involved a man who'd done some growing up and understood that anger was no useful response to what you didn't understand.

He nuzzled Johnny's cheek and then handed him back. 'Well that's the offer, Grace. And if you're not able to take it, I will have to live with that.' The end of the sentence finished in a whisper.

He bent down and scooped a hand over the side of her face before kissing her on the opposite cheek.

When he straightened, they looked at each other in silence while Johnny cooed to himself. 'Goodbye Grace.'

He left.

Soon after she heard a truck roar down the road, and then the wind took the sound away.

17

Johnny was almost eight months now and getting too big for the pram. Grace hoisted him out of it and onto her hip and left it near the gatehouse. She balanced him against her with one hand and in the other, carried a large yellow envelope that contained excellent references from Alf and Doctor Grey.

The hospital buildings seemed larger and more daunting than when she'd first visited, and the trailing branches of the willow tree in the central courtyard had been trimmed. They cascaded down in a waterfall of green leaves that never made it to the ground.

Near the visitors room she veered away from the entrance and took a path to the right that skirted around the men's building, following instructions to the administration block. At exactly two o'clock she knocked on the door of Matron Wood's office.

'Come in, Miss Anderson. Good to see you're a punctual person. We like that.' The woman stepped aside so Grace could enter. She was short and her head nested in a deep, white collar that ended at the edge of her shoulders. With no visible neck, she appeared truncated and Grace suppressed a giggle, for she couldn't help wondering if whoever had lopped the willow tree had seen to Matron as well.

The woman ignored the baby and ushered Grace to a chair in front of her desk, and then she sat behind it, lifting her shoulders back as she took charge.

'Your interest is pleasing, of course. It is laudable but most uncommon in someone who's had no training,' she began. She had the document in front of her that Grace had mailed two weeks ago, outlining her particulars. 'You've just turned nineteen, Miss Anderson. Don't you think you're a bit young to take this on?'

Grace had expected this question and her reply was well-rehearsed, starting with her time as a child in an institution and the domestic skills she'd been given, as well as her resulting appreciation of the need for structure, routine and predictability.

She gave a brief outline of the work she'd done at the orchard and guesthouse and the way she'd met the demands of other kitchen, laundry and outdoor work, as well as the reliability she'd demonstrated as cook and cleaner for Alf.

'You'll note in the reference provided by Mr Sturdy that although I am quite young I am a most responsible person, more than capable of hard work, and my performance is at a high standard,' she concluded.

If the Matron was impressed, her flinty face gave nothing away. 'You do realise, my dear, this is not just any challenge, so to speak. It's more of a calling, I would say. It takes a very understanding person to meet the needs of those who are not of sound mind.'

As Alf had suggested, knowing a great deal more than Grace about authority figures, she would need to show some humility at the right time in the interview.

Grace figured the time for that had arrived. 'Naturally, Matron, I am aware that I would have much to grasp and that I could not hope to understand all that you do with your many years of training and expertise. My genuine desire is to bring some care and kindness while gaining further knowledge about what it is to have a mind that cannot function properly.'

At this, the Matron unfolded her hands from the desk and leaned into the back of her chair. 'It would appear you've done quite a bit of thinking about this, Miss Anderson.'

'I have, Matron. This is not a girlish whim. I have had considerable discussions with the Superintendent and the doctor, who are both eminent men experienced in difficult matters and both of whom know me well. After talking it through, neither could see any reason to prevent me progressing my request.'

The discussions had been far livelier than she indicated to the Matron. Alf, for one, had been strongly opposed to the idea and had said so. 'For heaven's sake, Grace, this isn't something you do for a novelty for a week or so then forget about it. You're signing on for who knows how long!'

She'd never seen him so animated. If she hadn't known him so well, she would have been intimidated by his fury. But this was a rare occasion when she'd found the right words, the ones that best expressed how she was seeing the situation, and she was able to maintain her stand on the matter, wearing down his arguments one by one until eventually he came round.

In the thick of the heated debate with him, she'd had a brief moment where she'd considered telling Alf it was his very support and steadiness during the past year that had emboldened her to consider the scheme in the first place, but she let it pass.

The weeks after Tommy left for good had been hard. If desolation was the name of a place then Grace's cottage was in the town centre and all around gathered a yawning emptiness that no amount of work and manufactured tasks could fill.

In the hour before dark, with Johnny dozing off to sleep, she took to leaving him at home and walking to the end of the jetty, hoping none of the other women noticed because they would be on her case about not watching the baby. Standing above the restless river as treacly twilight came down and coated the view was the only time she could feel she had feet and hands and a heartbeat.

What had she done in all those days? She had no idea. Flour, eggs and some milk and sugar for pikelets on the griddle, that's what it was like. The rich possibilities of each morning tossed into a big bowl and stirred all day into a bland batter made by her mindless activity. Except that by evening she had nothing worth heating a griddle for, not a jot of plans for a future or anything solid that could feed her soul.

Perhaps, she had taken to thinking, this was the true definition of madness. Not the loss of contact with reality that had brought Jack Anderson undone but the dull repetition of daily nothingness that led a person to dissolve clean away.

And she, Grace Anderson, had been disappearing at a rapid pace.

After tackling Alf, it had taken another two weeks before she was ready to approach the doctor for a second reference and the necessary guarantees about medical treatment, and then a third week before Doctor Grey came to Low Head and she could corner him.

When she raised the subject, he took a long time removing his glasses, wiping the lenses, and then placing them on her table. 'What's brought this on then, lass?'

The question made it sound like she had an ailment rather than a determination about what must be done, but it was a reminder that it would be advantageous to talk with the doctor in terms of health and wholeness for him to understand.

'It's time for me to grow up, doctor. To accept who I am and what I must do so I can show my child what it is to be responsible.'

In truth, her decision hadn't been like that. There had been no cautious deliberation about options or an assessment of risk or anything else for that matter.

She had dragged herself in the door one evening with the light fading and lifted the kettle onto the stove before checking on Johnny. He was peaceful, one foot twitching a little in time with his shallow breath, utterly surrendered to sleep.

As she reached for the teapot, she hit whatever edge she'd been so desperately keeping at bay. The force of it knocked her against the table and she ignored the kettle spitting boiling water onto the stovetop because she had to crash onto a chair. In the most ordinary of moments, an unseen hand had whacked her and woken her up.

She could tell Doctor Grey none of this, of course. It was necessary to construct a more reasoned story for how she'd come to the decision.

As usual, he was calm and understanding. But he was a man of science and his analysis was less emotional than Alf's, requiring her to cover some new ground, particularly on the welfare of the baby.

The fact that she'd already garnered Alf's support added weight to her argument. She didn't mention Joyce, though she had sounded her out at length before asking either of the men for references.

Not only had Joyce seen Grace grow into a woman during her time at Low Head, she had the advantage of understanding the history of all that was involved. Alf did, too, but Grace knew it was Joyce who saw below the surface, to the dents and scars that lodged there and the way they caused her personality to seize up when movement was required.

Joyce had shared none of this; however, what she did say meant the world to Grace. 'It'll be hard, I don't doubt it. I've only known you a short while, but it doesn't take a genius to see you'll manage. You'll dig deep and you'll discover, as you did when you birthed Johnny, that all you have to do is keep going, keep doing your best.'

She told Grace a strange tale then, from her own childhood, about a wealthy friend of her mother's whose husband left for work one day at the local mine where he was manager, and never came home.

'Dropped dead in the cage when they were coming back up from examining a new shaft. In the first week after he'd gone, many people visited his wife at their grand home, drinking whiskey from crystal glasses and tea from delicate porcelain cups, surrounded by expensive furniture and paintings. Mum's friend was grief-stricken, but by the seventh day, her behaviour had changed. She started selling things and giving them away: clothes, kitchen utensils, bedding, the lot. Her grown-up sons had left after the funeral and Mum got a message to them to come back. They tried everything but couldn't persuade her to stop. She ended up selling the house and giving the proceeds to the boys. Left town in a cart with some basic possessions and crossed the nearby mountain range to live in a little shanty as a hermit. In the end, Mum understood.'

Joyce didn't elaborate on the point of the story, but Grace took it to be a parable on the need to go against the grain when your heart dictates it.

Doctor Grey was not inclined to tell long stories that might or might not have a point. He examined Grace's proposition and her need for a reference in minute detail, habituated as he was to seeking out all the facts and the physical signs in a patient before making a diagnosis.

She remained steadfast. Yes, it was a big step. No, there had been no pressure from any source to go down this path. Yes, Johnny would continue to be well cared for and she would, as usual, ensure everything he needed was provided, even if it meant arranging help.

After half an hour, the doctor collected his bag. 'You're taking a chance, Grace, but I'm satisfied you know what you're doing. I'm prepared to write you a reference and please remember, if ever I can assist in any way, let me know.'

He bowed as he left. He had never done that before but if it was intended as a gesture to honour her choice, she was touched.

Matron Woods was not inclined to pay homage to others, that much was clear to Grace as she submitted to the woman's grilling about health, motivation, expectations, and even her prospects of marriage.

'As you would appreciate, Miss Anderson, it is highly irregular to have a single woman make this kind of application. Let alone one ...' her voice trailed off as she looked down her nose at Johnny.

'I am mindful of my status, Matron, but have also been

to the library and read the latest annual report for the hospital, which outlines at some length the difficulties with overcrowding and shortages of staff. Surely my offer, which is well substantiated, can help take a little off the load.'

She appeared unconvinced and Grace felt she needed to act quickly to continue the small advantage she'd established.

'Of course the Superintendent, who is a long-time family friend, has indicated he will stay in touch and monitor the situation. I'm sure he would be comfortable in having you contact him should you have any concerns.'

The Matron brightened then; however, Johnny chose that precise moment to make it known that he'd had enough of sitting on Grace's lap and began whimpering.

'And the child, Miss Anderson? He needs his mother, I'm sure you would agree.'

'Nothing will change for my child, except that I may need assistance occasionally and I already have arrangements in place for when that occurs.' Feeling she had managed to win back the upper hand, Grace stood in readiness to thank Matron Woods for her time and ask when she might get a decision.

She didn't have to wait long. The Matron had made up her mind already.

'All is in order, Miss Anderson. The ward doctor will need to do his own interview in the morning and satisfy himself of your suitability, but we are generally of the same mind on such matters. Then there'll need to be some paperwork completed but it should all be tidied up within two weeks.'

By the time she'd collected the pram, Grace was already preparing a mental list of all that would need to be attended to before the fortnight was up.

18

Alf had driven south with her and Johnny. It seemed fitting that after all the years since he'd taken Jack away he should be the one to bring him back.

The ward doctor had assured Grace that her father was no longer prone to aggression, and she followed the medical man's advice, being careful to explain each new step in the process, starting with preparing Jack for leaving the hospital. She was relieved that the third time behind the high wall would be her last.

Jack showed no sign of recognising Alf but was cooperative as the older man helped him into the front seat of the car and explained that they were going to Low Head. When they stopped early afternoon for fish and chips at a roadside café, he seemed unsure about what to do with the food. He watched Alf and Grace eat with knives and forks and let his own meal get cold.

Grace went to ask for a paper bag so they could take some of the chips with them in case Jack got hungry but when she got back to the table, she found Alf had pulled the fish into pieces and Jack was eating it with his fingers, along with chips now drizzled with tomato sauce.

Back at the car, Alf suggested Jack sit in the back this time, and Grace saw him quietly lock the door before he went to the driver's seat. Jack dozed for much of the long drive home, stretched out along the seat with his jacket under his head and a large patch of dribble spreading over part of the sleeve.

Despite her bravado with the Matron and the ward doctor, Grace was nervous about what she'd done and how it would work out.

Taking him in was a selfish act, she wasn't kidding herself on that score. She was doing it for her own sanity. The only way she would ever lay the ghost of her father to rest would be to look the real man in the eye and give herself the chance to get to know him. That's if there was any more to know beyond the paper doll on the back seat.

She didn't raise the subject with Alf as the car passed the last of a string of towns and rattled through open grazing country. She couldn't have handled it if he'd expressed any doubts because she was so full of her own. They stayed on the safe ground of casual observations about the scenery or the white mile markers that came into view every fifteen minutes or so.

Johnny wasn't used to being cooped up in such a small space for a lengthy period and by the time they reached Campbell Town, with at least two hours travel to go, he started tossing himself about in Grace's arms and squealing sharply.

'Shall I stop so you can walk in the fresh air with the lad for a bit?' Alf asked.

Grace glanced over her shoulder at Jack, who continued sleeping. 'Best we keep going. I'll feed him and he'll go quiet,' she replied.

Alf drove for a few minutes more.

'I don't plan to interfere, you know that's not the way I work, but it's not always going to be easy juggling both their needs. I want you to remember that the little one is just starting out, but Jack's had his go so if it comes down to it, Johnny has to matter the most.'

Grace nodded. The message was disquieting but only because it was one she'd already been thinking.

Johnny had grown too big for the cradle and was in a cot now. Before she'd left Low Head, she and Joyce had moved the cot into Grace's bedroom. There was just enough space to jam it in the corner with the bed pushed against the wall. What had been the baby's room now had a borrowed single bed made of planks from a piece of Huon pine salvaged from a forest down south and on the floor, a small rug Grace had woven from rags.

She hadn't seen where Jack slept at the hospital and hoped the new arrangement would do. She would know soon enough.

THE FIRST MORNING, she placed a bowl of porridge before Jack and asked if he preferred sugar or honey. He had the same look on his face as when she'd offered him the gift at the hospital except there was no attendant to help her decipher it.

'What is it, Jack?' she asked as gently as she could.

He began shaking his head and she feared he would get worked up. 'Why haven't they rung the bell? It can't be porridge time if they haven't rung the bell.'

She didn't dare touch him by way of reassurance in case he reacted. Instead, she picked Johnny up and sat back at the table. 'See Jack, we have a baby in this place and that's why we don't use bells at mealtimes, because they might frighten him.'

He stopped shaking his head, though the confusion remained on his face.

'There won't be bells anymore at mealtimes. I'll be letting you know from now on when it's time to eat.'

He looked at her but this time he was studying her face intently, his head to one side. 'Of course, Amy. You were always a good cook. I knew you'd be back when the baby was fit to travel again. It was a long time you were in Hobart with your family.'

Grace tried to set him right. 'It's Grace you're speaking to...'

'I know, love, she's a bonny one. Look at that smile.'

Johnny lunged towards his mother's porridge and Grace swiftly intercepted his hand.

When she glanced back up, Jack was reaching for the sugar. He gave the porridge a liberal coating of it before tucking in.

Grace ate her breakfast and let her father be, not bothering to correct the misunderstanding. Who was to say what world each of us inhabited and which was better. She'd had dreams over the years that were more vivid and felt more real than the life awaiting when she woke.

When it was time to leave, she took Jack out the front door and pointed up the hill to the lighthouse. 'See the white cottage next to it? That's where I'll be with the baby if there's anything you need.'

She led him back inside and showed him the clock. 'I'll be back at noon to fix you some food. See, when both hands get up here.' She tapped the top of the clock.

He seemed to understand, and by the time she'd readied herself and Johnny to go to work, he had swung one of the chairs around and was sitting near the window, staring out.

'Remember, Jack, I'm just up there in the cottage if you need anything.'

He continued looking out the window and gave a faint nod. She left him sitting there, quiet and soft.

He wasn't there when she hurried down the hill with Johnny at lunchtime. She was on her way to check outside, panic rising, when she heard a clatter from Jack's bedroom. What she saw through the doorway was more caged beast than man. He'd tipped over the chair and she couldn't tell if it had been accidental or deliberate but now he was rocking on the edge of the bed.

The short, rhythmic jerks of one heel had bunched up the rug, scuffing it towards him, while the opposite leg strained forward so that its boot pushed the rug away. The pushing and pulling were applied with equal force as though Jack was trying to run away and simultaneously withdraw into hiding.

Grace saw the tension and cut off the impulse to go to him. Such a movement from her might disturb whatever equilibrium he was battling to maintain.

What had she done, thinking she could snatch him away from the life he'd known? A mind diverted from its normal course could not be predicted to follow the usual flow of cause and effect. She'd left him alone and in the void of it, he was now untethered.

The thought stirred her into action. She propped the baby on a pillow in the corner and cut two thick slices of bread, covering each with cheese and a generous spread of tomato chutney.

She placed the two plates on the table and spoke in a voice more calm than she felt. 'Jack, come to the kitchen. It's time to eat and I'm waiting at the table to eat with you.'

Silence.

She tapped the knife a few times on the plate, so it

sounded like mealtime. The bed creaked, then all was silent. As she pushed back her chair to go to him, he appeared in the doorway and came over to take his seat.

'When you've had your bread and cheese, I'll make us some tea.' She was trying for simple acts of giving shape to his world. She hoped it would work.

At least he hadn't tried to wander off in her absence. That much was a relief. It would not do, though, to leave him to his own devices and she couldn't help scolding herself for not thinking it through. When she glanced out the window, she could swear the reflection of shifting light showed the Matron's disapproving face.

She stayed as long as she could before returning to Alf's cottage. She unpegged the washing from the line and folded it, put fresh sheets on the bed, diced carrots and turnips and set them aside with a note giving Alf instructions on how to cook them to go with the steak and kidney pie she'd made that morning.

As she worked, her mind turned over the situation with Jack. It was impossible to leave him sitting in her cottage for five or six hours a day. She needed to explore what might give him an interest and a routine.

Back home, she opened the mesh door on the meat safe and took out a couple of pasties Joyce had made. Jack had been waiting at the table, frequently rubbing his hands together but otherwise more settled than earlier.

They ate the pasties cold. It wasn't ideal but the oven had no heat because she hadn't been willing to risk giving him responsibility for tending the fire in her absence. Though she'd set the kindling alight as soon as she'd arrived home and it was burning brightly, she didn't want to distress him by delaying his meal when he was clearly expecting to eat right then.

She picked up their plates and went to get the teapot before lifting the kettle onto the stove. 'What time do you go to bed, Jack?' What had possessed her not to have thought to ask such questions from the asylum staff?

'Before lights out,' he answered, giving her no information at all.

She was at a loss. It had been so easy with Johnny, sensing his natural rhythm and responding with what he might need; a give and take to determine what worked and what didn't. The baby, though, had no patterns to unlearn and he did not have the size or strength to do any harm.

She built up the fire with two small logs and soon the heat had the kettle singing.

'Nine o'clock's a good bedtime, Jack, don't you reckon?' She ignored the lack of an answer. 'Yes, nine o'clock it will be.'

After they'd drunk their tea, she filled the tin tub with the remaining hot water from the kettle to wash the day's dishes.

She put a tea towel on the table in front of him and as she washed each bowl, plate and cup, she handed it to him to dry. He didn't mount any objection and did as he was asked. That was at least something, she thought, that he might cope with instructions framed as requests.

Next morning, she guided him to the small yard behind her quarters and showed him the thyme and sage she'd planted in the corner. She explained how she wanted a vegetable patch and dragged her boot across the ground to indicate where the boundaries might go.

He appeared to listen as she outlined what she'd found she could grow at Alf's cottage in salt-laden air: root vegetables, cabbages and pumpkins in autumn; green peas, broad beans, tomatoes in spring and summer. She took him into the laundry and showed him the new spade and garden fork she hadn't had a chance to use, and the shelf with packets of seeds.

He looked perplexed. Then she remembered what the doctor had said, about Jack's ability to perform practical tasks but only if the demands were simple.

'Each day, do you think you could dig a row or two for the veggie garden?

He nodded.

It was enough for now and she made a mental note to give him one specific task each morning.

He was slow and if there was a hiccup and he couldn't see his way around the problem, he would wait until Grace returned to suggest the solution. One day he'd been part way through planting radishes when he'd run out of seeds. It didn't occur to him to check the laundry shelf for more. Another day the spout broke off the watering can and he was unable to grasp that he could pour water without the spout.

Despite his lack of capacity to initiate, he worked in the garden each day and soon it was a decent size. He gave no indication that he enjoyed gardening, but Grace noticed that once he'd eaten breakfast he would pull on his boots and set to work. She watched him on her day off, working in bursts interspersed with long periods leaning on the spade and looking out to the river.

He showed no interest whatsoever in interacting with the other men, which was a blessing because it meant he stayed in the cottage or garden. Where others might have felt hemmed in, it was as if all the years of confinement behind the wall had delivered safety in edges and borders. Sometimes he walked the length of the fence or paced the cottage as far as the front door, but that was as far as he went.

Alf came by once a week and poured them a beer, and when it was sunny, the two men sat on the back step and drank in silence. If it was windy or cold, they took up positions at the table, Alf telling an occasional tale about the weather or something he'd heard on the radio. Grace wasn't sure if the stories were meant for her benefit or to help Alf pass the time. They washed over Jack as though he wasn't even there.

'It's a sorry state of affairs. He doesn't understand who I am,' she said to Alf one afternoon as she walked him to the gate when he was leaving.

'He doesn't seem to know who I am either,' Alf said. 'But that doesn't mean he can't enjoy my company.'

She was inclined to agree with Alf, she thought later, in that Jack seemed to have become accustomed to her and Johnny. He was more settled in the arrangement than Grace herself. She hadn't known what to expect, but clearly she must have expected something because whatever it was had been too much.

It was rare for Jack to talk and when he did, he continued to address her and Johnny as the wife and child he'd known. After a couple of weeks, it no longer hurt as much to have him speak in that way, not once she heard the love in his voice for Amy and the baby Grace.

When she'd been that small girl in the rescue home, Jack had not been able to claim her or provide care; however, she had found a way to claim her father. And that was enough, she told herself.

In the early hours the following morning, she woke to the sound of a dog barking. As the fog of sleep cleared, she staggered to her feet and reached into the cot beside her. The harsh, prolonged coughs belonged to Johnny.

He was distressed and when she leaned over to pick him up, his skin was hot and clammy.

She soaked a cloth in cold water, wrung it out and wiped him down in an effort to reduce his temperature. When she put him to the breast, he sucked vigorously at first, and then he pulled away after swallowing and cried fitfully between the bouts of coughing.

She walked the floor with him for a couple of hours, holding him upright on her shoulder in the only position he seemed to tolerate. At first light she placed him on the table to examine him more clearly and was alarmed at the bluish tinge of his skin.

She bundled him in his blanket and ran with him in her arms, not bothering with the pram. Within minutes she was knocking on Joyce's door. Will had finished the night shift and turned off the light a short time earlier and he was the one to greet her.

'I wouldn't be bothering you except it's an emergency. Can I speak to Joyce please?'

He stepped aside. 'Come in lass, come in'.

She could hardly get her breath. 'Best I don't. Johnny's sick and it could be diphtheria. I don't want to put your kids at risk.'

At that, Joyce appeared. She took one look at Johnny and sent her husband to fetch Alf. 'He needs to get to hospital straight away,' was all she said.

Johnny's coughing had slowed and he felt limp in Grace's arms. 'Please Johnny, please,' she whispered to him while she waited for Alf to bring the car.

Joyce was at her elbow. 'Sure he's but a scrap of a boy

but he's strong, Grace, he's strong.'

Grace, however, was too far gone in the panic to acknowledge her friend's reassurance. She swayed, shifting her weight from one foot to another and back again in a useless attempt to soothe the baby and the hope that it might help calm her. It made not an ounce of difference to either.

In the car, Alf made no conversation or comment but seized the steering wheel and drove, the sedan attacking the corners and going full throttle on the straights. Grace braced herself and Johnny against the passenger door.

Near George Town, she lost her nerve and pleaded with Alf to stop at Doctor Grey's surgery and wake him in his private rooms at the rear, but Alf wouldn't be swayed.

'We've gotta get him to Launceston as quick as we can. It's hospital he needs, Grace.'

She was too wretched even for tears. The baby's face was hot as she stroked his cheeks, so she drew back the blanket from his chest. It was painful to loosen her hold when all she wanted was to clutch at him, stop him sinking further away.

Mr Jacques had phoned ahead but the on-call doctor had still not arrived when Grace carried Johnny into the hospital waiting room. She forced her mind away from her boy and thought instead of Jack waking to an empty house, confronted by the departure of predictability. She hoped Joyce would have the chance to get to him, give him reassurance and keep him in some semblance of his routine.

Alf stayed in the waiting room with her, telling her what she already knew, that as Superintendent, if it was diphtheria he would need to ensure the lighthouse, cottages and pilot station were quarantined immediately. The real reason he didn't leave was in the tightness of his face and the restlessness of one foot, the heel jiggling on the floor. She had a fleeting thought that perhaps he'd once sat in the same waiting room with Mrs Sturdy and his own child.

Grace had collapsed into begging the nurse to do something by the time the doctor arrived. He was younger than Doctor Grey, and whether it was his manner or the result of one call-out too many during the night, he quickly dispensed with any courtesies and brushed Alf aside as he led Grace and the baby into a side room.

He began examining Johnny's mouth and throat and testing his reflexes. For the first time since his birth, the boy looked fragile on the large examination table. His limbs jerked occasionally and he lacked the energy to cough, rasping a little and labouring in the attempt to drag in air.

'How long's he been like this? Has he been in contact with any other child that has these symptoms? Is there any history of respiratory problems? What's his general health been like?'

The hail of questions went on, but all Grace desired was to hear some answers.

The doctor finished his checks and directed that Johnny be admitted for observation and to get his fever down.

'Is it diphtheria?' Grace asked, knowing it could kill or at the very least leave a child with a weak heart.

'Too early to tell. His throat does seem to have a grey coating and it's definitely sore. There's also some evidence of swelling in his glands. We need to keep a close eye on him.'

In most instances the hospital sent the mother away if a child was admitted; however, as Grace was still breastfeeding Johnny, he announced that she would be spared the separation.

Before Johnny was taken to the ward, the doctor gave instructions to Alf. 'If you can, don't let anyone leave the pilot station site until we can get a handle on this. We won't officially quarantine you until we have a definite diagnosis.'

Grace followed the nurse. She was ridiculously fresh-faced for the hour of the day, not long out of her training she said, chattering away. Though her attempts at providing distraction were well meant, Grace couldn't bear it and shut her down.

The nurse stripped off Johnny's clothes and sponged his listless body while Grace stood by uselessly, praying silently to the God that had never figured in her life. The begging was obscene but it was all she had left. *Let him live. I will never ask for another thing, but let him live.*

She was encouraged to offer him the breast frequently for fear he would become dehydrated. He barely had the strength to latch on but, young as he was, the survival instinct was still strong and he managed to swallow three or four mouthfuls each time.

The nurse wheeled in a trolley with an electric fan and switched it on. Whether it was the strangeness of the sound or the moving air, Johnny was unhappy and bleated miserably.

The doctor returned a few hours later and placed a thermometer under the baby's arm. 'He seems a little cooler. That's promising.'

Grace continued to lift Johnny from the cot every hour

in an attempt to get him to drink and, she hoped, reassure him with her touch. The nurse came often with a syringe she used to squirt small amounts of sterile water into his mouth. In between he dozed, restless and pale against the white sheet.

Through the night, Grace watched the clock above the nurses station grind out the minutes and then the hour. If she kept her eyes on it, the hands stalled for however long she stared and any halting progress was kept for the moments when she turned her back.

She was exhausted and desperate for sleep by three in the morning but terrified that if she let herself doze in the chair, Johnny might slip away. She straightened her spine and pressed her feet firmly onto the floor. She would keep watch. She wouldn't let him go.

The hands had done another circuit of the clock when her head became so heavy she leaned forward and let it rest in her hands, eyelids closed. Darkness began rising from the floor, tiny pinpricks of light floating in the black, dancing in sparkles on a surface that was no longer empty space but water that was rising steadily, up and on.

She bolted upright, eyes wide open and reached out to place a hand on Johnny. He seemed to be sleeping, but under her fingers, his abdomen was ragged in its rise and fall. When she could no longer support the weight of her arm, she slumped back in the chair.

When next she opened her eyes, the cot was empty.

19

In the days after leaving hospital, she kept reliving the sight of the bare cot and every time she did, it was a punch to her gut.

That awful morning, fear had intensified the force of gravity and she'd struggled to get to her feet. A voice had been calling 'nurse, nurse' and she was part way down the corridor before she'd realised it was her own.

She must have started shouting because a firm pair of hands had grasped her by the shoulders and from instinct, she began fighting what felt like an attack from behind.

It was the nurse on the new shift, saying her name. 'Settle down, Grace. Stay calm.'

In the confusion, she'd shaken off the woman and started to run.

'Come back, Johnny's in here, he's in here.'

When Grace looked back, the nurse was gesturing to a nearby door.

Numb, she retraced her steps and entered the room. It had a sink and a stainless steel bench on one wall and on the bench was a baby's bath. Next to it was a bundle in a white towel.

A second nurse held it up. 'His fever broke. We'll get him dressed then he needs to be fed.'

Grace took him from her immediately — there was no question she could wait. His eyes were still dull but he was searching her face, and for the first time in twenty-four hours she could see he knew it was her.

Tonsillitis, the doctor had said on his round, often confused with diphtheria in the first day or so.

It still hurt, even now, to feel how lightly balanced her son's life had been. He was recovering well; however, any sense of certainty she'd gained in recent times had been shaken to the core.

Jack, too, was unsettled. Joyce, with her own busy family to tend, had done her best to keep him fed and in a routine each day. Despite her efforts, he'd reacted to their absence with anxious pacing and an unwillingness to work. He'd developed a restless shaking in his hands and when he sat, his feet tapped and jerked. It was painful to watch him out of kilter.

For the first two days, he gave no sign to acknowledge their return. He ate whatever food she placed in front of him but kept his head bent and eyes fixed on the floor. Any comments or questions met with no resistance but instead dissolved in the air around him as though they hadn't been uttered at all.

Alf had told her to take the week off and she was grateful for it. She needed the time to coax Jack back into the garden and Johnny into his normal feeding and sleep pattern. The baby adapted easily, soon settling into an hour and a half of sleep each morning and again in the afternoon, and then sleeping from late evening until just before dawn.

She tried talking to Jack but it was a fruitless effort and he remained consumed by restless tics and shaking. Desperate, she opened the back door one morning while he sat at the table eating breakfast and went out to fetch the spade. She held it up in front of him, a magic talisman that might transform him back to his old self. He ignored it and when he finished his porridge returned to sit and fidget on his bed.

In the end she resorted to a lie.

She went to him and touched him lightly on the shoulder. 'Me and the baby, we're here, Jack, we're okay. You've had a bad dream but you're awake now, look.' She waved her other hand towards the living area of the cottage. 'Come out and see the baby. Take my hand, we'll go together.' She reached for his fingers but he pulled both hands together and clasped them on his lap. She stood and walked away. She was exhausted and had run out of ideas.

She was outside the bedroom before she noticed the soft shuffling behind. She thought of the beaten pup at the orchard: one false move and she'd frighten him away. She ignored the urge to turn and look at Jack, instead picking up Johnny and chatting with him in a playful way.

She carried the baby out to the yard, leaving the back door ajar, and collected the spade from where she'd propped it against the laundry wall. She carried it to the veggie patch and jammed it upright into soft soil on the edge, then sat on the back step, clapping her hands in time as she sang to the boy.

Diddle, diddle, dumpling, my son John,
Went to bed with his trousers on;
One shoe off, and the other shoe on,
Diddle, diddle, dumpling, my son John.

She'd almost finished the first verse when she caught sight of Jack out the corner of her eye. He was standing behind her and looking towards the garden. 'If you want to keep turning over that row, Jack, I'll get the kettle on and I can call you when it's time for a piece of cake and a cuppa.'

He stepped aside to let her and the baby through the doorway, and she deliberately delayed the process of changing Johnny's nappy and settling him in the cot for his sleep. When she glanced back into the yard, Jack was digging slowly, pausing to lean on the spade between turning each clump of soil.

She was pleased to be free of the heavy hours of worry at the hospital, and for the remaining days off, yoked herself to activity: catching up on washing, rocking Johnny in the pram while she talked Jack through each task in the yard, preparing them simple meals, checking the boy's breathing every few minutes while he slept.

Joyce dropped in for a brief visit, delighted to see Johnny balanced on Grace's lap and sucking on an arrowroot biscuit. 'You've got Jack back on the shovel, then? He acted up a bit about you being gone.'

Grace nodded and thanked her friend for all she'd done. 'He's starting to settle but it's hard to say if it'll stick. It's been a lot of change after all those years he spent with none.'

Ruby's mum popped in to see how Johnny was but that was the extent of visitors for the week. She was glad of it. Her body felt like it was floating and she needed the time to get back to ground. At night, she lay in bed schooling her mind to find the heaviness in her limbs that would bear her down to sleep.

The following Monday she went back to work. Jack was unhappy when it was time for her to leave and took some convincing that she and Johnny would be back at lunchtime. When she returned, she was glad to see him in the garden. After they'd eaten, he again resisted her departure. She changed tack and suggested he walk with them to Alf's cottage and weed the garden there.

He shook his head. 'I'm not going near the light.'

The statement was emphatic, accompanied by a sharp tilt of the head. It said everything she'd been blind to since he'd arrived. Jack Anderson may have been an asylum inmate but that obscured who he really was. The man who stood before her was no aberration. In the logic of his life, he was sane; an ordinary man who'd ruptured after one too many body blows.

She'd been looking at him through the eyes of a needy child. She'd known the despair of being parted from Mary and the baby girl, for sure, but the sorrow and wounding when she'd thought she'd lost Johnny had been on another scale. The kind of scale that she might use as a grown woman to measure some of Jack's pain.

Her father, for now she felt he was just that, had taken all he could and then no more. He hadn't failed her in the heartless way she'd always thought. He'd gone under because his heart had been ripped apart.

She couldn't say she loved him as she watched him anew, though that might eventually come, but she felt gentler. He, for his part, responded to the change. Within ten minutes she had him working with the spade, digging a small pit where they could layer any excess carrots and turnips with earth to store them for use in winter.

She left him bending to the task and took Johnny to Alf's cottage to finish off the chores.

Jack was on her mind all afternoon. If his agitation escalated, she mightn't be able to manage. The idea of locking him back up in New Norfolk was too hard to bear. She gave up on the plan to make Alf beef stew, instead peeling a pot of potatoes and leaving him a few lamb chops to fry so she could finish early. She hastily wheeled the baby home.

She needn't have worried. Weeks earlier, she'd suggested that Jack stack some logs of wood against the fence for a makeshift seat and when she opened the gate, he was sitting quietly on it and surveying his afternoon's work.

On the Sunday, she invited him to join her for a picnic at East Beach, with no expectation he'd agree, so when he said yes she had to stop herself from exclaiming. She didn't bother to tell him it was a celebration of sorts, that it marked a little over a year since she'd arrived at Low Head.

She was tempted to ask Joyce if she would like to join them with her brood but decided against it. The noise and activity would be too much for Jack.

She made a batch of savoury scones and packed some in a basket with bread, cheese, ripe pears and a large bottle of home-made ginger beer. As they were leaving, she thought he might offer to carry the basket but he didn't, though he was agreeable to taking it from her when asked.

While Jack was his usual incommunicative self, Johnny sat up in the pram and despite a little bouncing on the uneven sections of the track, cheerily surveyed all they passed on the way to the beach, chirping when a bush, a gull or even a section of fence pleased him.

It was cooler than she'd expected but she shook out the picnic blanket on the edge of the boobiallas, which provided shelter for the three of them as they sat. Johnny had begun to crawl a few days earlier but so far could only manage a few motions before he'd collapse. He tried his new skills on the blanket and had reached the edge when the limits of his strength gave out and he dropped face down in the sand. Grace burst into laughter as she scooped him up and brushed off his face. The baby was too stunned to cry.

Jack showed no reaction, though he watched intently while Grace soothed Johnny. She caught herself wondering how it might be if Jack was a proper grandfather, interacting with the boy — cuddling him, playing with him, showing him the world. She was indulging in fantasy, she knew, and it was no more helpful than a dog turd stuck to her shoe. At least he was with them, sharing a picnic. When she glanced at her father, he was munching his way through a scone and staring out across the sea.

After an hour, the wind picked up and she gathered the food into the basket and left it on the beach while she carried Johnny to the pram on the edge of the track. She folded the picnic blanket and placed it over Johnny's feet. As she did, her father came up behind her, the basket in his hands.

It was a natural thing to say, an instinctive reaction to his first display of initiative. 'Thank you, Dad.'

It didn't seem to matter to him because he ignored what she said, but the sound of it eased a tight place under her ribs.

Alf visited later in the afternoon and sat quietly with Jack while Grace washed up and packed away the picnic things. The mood in her cottage wrapped around them, comfortable as leather on well-worn boots. It stayed that way into the evening, after Alf had gone home.

Next morning, she steeled herself to tussle with her father about leaving for work, but he was back to his usual self, slogging through his porridge, and then heading out to the garden as though there'd never been any disruption.

THE DAY HAD passed quickly. Johnny was asleep and Jack had gone to bed.

The postman would collect the grocery order tomorrow. She pulled out the writing pad and finished her list before tearing off the sheet and folding it in an envelope. She printed her name neatly on the front and propped it on the mantelpiece, then went to check on the baby.

Back at the table, she sat transfixed by the blank page on the upturned pad while her mind churned through the past year. She thought of Beattie, how she'd been the one wise enough to share how life zigged and then zagged, but Grace had been too careless to hear. She would get in touch; let her know how she fared.

The times with Beattie in the guesthouse kitchen belonged to a comet that burned itself up as it shot through space. Since then she'd gained a son and a father, too. She was the one who'd chosen to care for them both; clumsy, blind choices — who knows, maybe made by a fool.

Tomorrow, next week, next year the pair of them could be gone, swept away in one unholy torrent like the family she might've had. She felt it keenly, the slim hold she had on the future, the way small acts of power sometimes mattered and sometimes didn't. Saw her younger self braced at the ferry rail, clinging to the only substance she had, the wonky belief that all it would take to turn herself into someone worthwhile was a willingness to work and a strength of will.

She was on her way to becoming someone but it wasn't down to any talent or determination she might have. Like learning to read her fractured father, she'd need more time to decipher the woman that circumstances were continuing to reveal. If it took decades, that would have to do.

She was afraid, that much was certain. But for all the fear, she had learnt she could rely on two things wherever she was. They weren't much, though in time she might learn to be grateful for the fact that they were there at all. She had the ability to stumble on, and the intent to try her best.

Everything had brought her here; every bad thing, each small surprising joy. She thought she would break, and she had, but there were different ways to fall. Her father had broken down, some pieces scattering, never to be found. She had broken apart, not a clean cut — she wished it had been that — but a slow ravaging that had worn her out at first then opened her, leaving the ragged edges you'd find with a blunt can opener. Would there be healing? She hoped so, but the future was too difficult to contemplate. It was enough to deal with the present.

It was quiet in the cottage, not even the sound of a dog barking or a possum skittering on the roof. Each tick of the clock pressed the silence a little deeper until it settled on her head and shoulders, casting a peaceful cloak.

Bedtime. She picked up the pen to put it back in the drawer. Her hand paused and she held the pen in front of her for the longest time, staring at it as though she'd never seen one before. When she lowered it, she dipped it into the bottle of blue ink then pressed it firmly to the paper to stop it from shaking. She had no idea what to write but what mattered was to make a start.

Dear Tommy …

Author's Note

This novel is a work of fiction; although, an historic event triggered the ideas that led to the creation of Grace and her story.

On the night of 13 August 1907, the steamship *Kawatiri* ran aground in treacherous conditions at Hells Gates, the narrow access to an isolated harbour on the west coast of Australia's island state, Tasmania. The ship had made it across the bar but was still in rough waters when it foundered within sight of the lighthouse on Entrance Island, inside the harbour mouth.

I was researching stories for a tourism client when I came across entries referring to the shipwreck in the original lighthouse logbooks — sparse, handwritten notes that sent me in search of newspaper articles and other records of the tragedy.

The accounts of the Hooper lighthouse family were touching, showing how powerfully the direction of our lives can change in an instant. Although I walked away from the Archives Office, it was impossible to leave behind the vivid images playing in my mind.

The assistant lighthouse keeper's wife, Marian Hooper, was on board the ship with her two young sons and not expected back so soon from the capital city of Hobart. She and the children were thrown from the lifeboat within reach of safety and swept away, while her husband Robert stood helplessly on the bridge of the light tower. At the coronial inquiry, he reported hearing her desperate shouts to be saved while he could do nothing.

Unlike in the novel, both Hooper children drowned.

The stewardess and two other children also lost their lives.

Robert Hooper, known as Jack, was given brief leave of absence for the funerals, but the thirty-year-old was back at work within days, watching over the waters that swallowed his family. Within a month, and only after the bodies of his wife and one son had been found, he had packed up his furniture and transferred to Low Head, where he worked at the Tamar Leading Lights.

He went on to marry the nineteen-year-old daughter of the head lighthouse keeper, Doris Lambert. After their wedding, the pair were transferred to remote Goose Island. A little more than a year after their marriage, Doris died after giving birth to twins, who also did not survive. Any other similarities to the lighthouse keeper end there.

Robert Hooper went on to other lighthouse postings but does not appear to have remarried.

The rugged, often inaccessible coastline of Tasmanian meant that most of the early lighthouse keepers and their families lived in isolation. Low Head was an exception and the co-location of lighthouse employees and the pilot service saw a self-sufficient community develop over time.

The lighthouse service and pilot service were operated under separate structures by the Commonwealth of Australia and the Launceston Marine Board, with site responsibilities discharged by a lighthouse superintendent and a pilot-in-charge. For the purposes of the novel, I have given the lighthouse superintendent greater authority over the site than would have been the case.

Anna Housego

Anna has been writing all her working life. Originally a journalist, she worked at an outback pub, did a stint as a political adviser and had her own communications consultancy for two decades. She now writes fiction full-time.

She grew up in a wilderness town full of colourful characters, sparking her love of stories. These days she's a mother and grandma and lives near the Southern Ocean in Tasmania, a small island below the south-eastern corner of Australia.

She is also the author of *The Way To Midnight (2018)*, the page-turning novel about a shattering 1930s event hidden for a generation. It is based on the true story of her aunt, erased from family history after her mysterious death.

Get your free download of *Disgrace: Uncovering a Family Secret* at www.annahousego.com

Anna welcomes and greatly appreciates your support: **Like her page:**

 @annahousegoauthor

Follow her:

 @annahousego

Post a review on Goodreads, Amazon or site of purchase.